LOOK
FOR ME

Muchas
Gracias !

Douglas Kirk

Douglas Kirk

ii

*What a difference
a little kiss made.*

Written by Douglas Kirk
Edited by Lori Kirk
Cover Photo by Douglas Kirk
Cover Design by Kelsie Kirk
Author Photo by Kelsie Kirk

10 9 8 7

Distributed by Morton Falls Publishing Company

ISBN-13: 978-0-934-27916-1
ISBN-10: 0-934279-16-0

Hier ruht in Frieden
LILLY
Tochter von
HERMANN UND EMMA
BARTLES
GEB.
JULI 22, 1894
GEST.
SEPT. 5, 1899

Wenn kleine Himmels erben
In ihrer Unschuld sterben
So büßt man sie nicht ein.

This series is dedicated to
Lilly Bartels, whose role in a
paranormal experience Oct. 24, 2008
at the Startz cemetery, resulted in
discussion that lead to
the premise of this story.

Chapter 1

October 24, 2008
Canyon Lake, Texas

When you first meet a person, you know nothing about them. You can look at them from a distance and notice a few things, but it takes a while to really understand who they are. That is, unless you meet under extraordinary circumstances.

Startz Cemetery was a small plot on a seldom traveled country road tucked in the middle of gently rolling hills in an out-of-the-way part of the state in southern Texas. There were a few dozen graves there, some dating back 150 years. Somebody took care of the cemetery, but not often, because the weeds had grown up on the fence line and around the majestic oaks that shielded the headstones from the sun. Grey moss hung from the branches and cast an eerie light across the open area as the sun set each day. Long shadows made dark lines across the spaces between the plots where people had stood to mourn the deaths of their loved ones.

The sun was pretty much down to the horizon and falling fast when Wallace Larame trudged across the field and slumped back against the stump of an oak that had been cut and fashioned into a place to sit. Wallace really didn't care if it would be comfortable. He didn't plan to be there long.

He was pretty tired. Not physically, but he had a weariness about him that people only get when they've given up--struggled and hoped against all odds only to be beaten down to the point of futility. A man can take a lot of abuse in his life, a lot of failures, a lot of disrespect, a lot of rejection, but there comes a point where fighting just seems pointless. Wallace was at that place in his life, and so he pulled out a .45 pistol and held it near the temple of his head.

There was a little grey in his once all-brown hair, and the skin that looked young for so long had begun to show its age. Wallace wasn't old, but his dreams had turned to nightmares, and he figured there wasn't enough time left to sort it all out. His muscles weren't what they used to be, nor was his stamina. But it wasn't that which propelled him to his decision, the ulti-mate decision. As a psychologist trained to help people, he was overwhelmed with problems, other people's problems. He knew he couldn't fix things. He tried. But the small victories did not make up for the huge losses. He really just didn't want to do it anymore. He was tired of getting up in the morning, tired of pretending to be someone he wasn't, tired of being optimistic for everyone else.

He could not be of benefit to peo-ple any longer, and his depression was deep-seated. Pulling a trigger just seemed so easy.

But then, as he sat there thinking over his life, gun ready, he had a hard time doing it. Part of him said go ahead. Part said just squeeze the trigger and do it. The other part was afraid, a little fight still left in him, but not much.

"What are you doing?" came a woman's voice out of the near darkness.

Wallace hesitated, looked about and saw no one. He relaxed his hold on the gun temporarily while his tired brown eyes scanned for the source of the voice.

He heard crickets as the sun disappeared below the meadow in the distance. Wallace gripped the gun tighter and brought it closer to his skin.

"What do you figure you are going to do, save the taxpayer money?" asked a girl a fraction of his age. She had had a flat tire and was walking to town when she saw Wallace's car parked at the cemetery. She was going to ask him for a ride, but when she saw the gun, all that changed. Circumstances happen that way sometimes. Coincidence? Maybe. But maybe not. Maybe fate is real. Maybe certain things were meant to be. Maybe Lauri Walters was supposed to find this guy in the cemetery and stop him and thereby change his life and maybe hers.

Wallace looked around to see the woman step out of the shadows. Her hair hung down to her waist, and he noticed right off how it looked almost gold in the waning light.

"What do you think you are going to do with that gun?" she asked persistently.

Wallace lowered the weapon slightly.

"Well, until you showed up I was planning to kill myself. Doesn't that seem pretty obvious to you?"

"That's not a very good plan."

"Who are you, my guardian angel?"

Lauri stepped closer. She was tall, and shapely, standing there in jeans with high heels.

"No, but I don't really think it is

such a good idea to shoot yourself."

"Why not?"

Lauri moved quickly to Wallace's side and knelt and put her head next to his. Wallace flinched.

"You know if you pull that trigger," she said, "with a gun that big the bullet is going to go right through your head and you're going to kill me, too." She paused. "Are you going to do it?"

"I don't think that is a good idea," said Wallace.

"You see? We're getting somewhere. Now we both agree it is a bad idea."

Wallace lowered the gun and brushed Lauri away from him. She rolled back but as soon as Wallace released his grip she put her head right back against his.

"You know if you do this," she said, "the local paper will have a heck of a story. I can see the headlines now. *Murder Suicide In Lovers' Pact, Two Dead At Cemetery.*"

Wallace placed the gun on the ground and released it.

"That's pretty funny," he said, with a tiny smile on his cheek.

Lauri sat back, cross-legged on the ground next to Wallace.

"It's getting better already. We agree it's a bad idea for both of us to die here and you're laughing about it."

Wallace uttered a quiet laugh and tilted his head toward the ground.

"That is pretty funny, you have to admit," said Lauri. *"Two Dead At Cemetery.* Look around here, there's probably more than two people in all these graves so the paper would be wrong. They would have to write *Murder Suicide In Lovers' Pact, Fifty Dead At Cemetery.* Now that would bring out the tourists. Damn, can you imagine?"

Wallace smiled genuinely.

"Who the hell are you?"

"Well, sir, it looks like I *am* your guardian angel. Got a flat on my car and I was going to ask you for a ride. You can't help me if I don't help you."

Wallace looked out at the grave markers and scanned them one-by-one.

Lauri studied his face. It looked

like there had been a tear in his eye, but she wasn't sure in the darkened light.

"Why are you here, really?" she asked softly.

Wallace turned toward her. He looked at her eyes. They were expressive and so large.

"I was going to kill myself," he said assertively.

"Well now that you're not, what are you doing?" asked Lauri leaning toward the man.

"I don't know. You sorta messed up my plans."

"So are you going to thank me and give me a ride?"

"I suppose I should, except I'm not sure if you've done a good deed or just delayed the inevitable."

"What? Death? Death is not the end. People go on, you know."

"Yeah, so we're told. But that doesn't make living any easier."

"What do you have to be so miserable about?" asked Lauri as she reached out and gently touched Wal-

- 8 -

lace's hand. Wallace retracted his hand slightly. Lauri reached farther and took hold of his hand.

"Who are you?" he asked.

"What does that matter? We're two people sitting in the middle of a cemetery in the dark. How bad can your life be?"

"Well, I'd say it is looking up."

"Wow," said Lauri. "So you're pretty far down. And you thought killing yourself here would save all the trouble of somebody finding the body and a medical examiner putting you in the freezer for awhile and then a funeral where you'd end up here anyway?"

"Something like that."

"You see," said Lauri, "that already tells me that you are a smart guy. Why would such a smart guy kill himself? Are you a stockbroker or something? You know that the DOW just up and crashed, didn't it? People lost billions!" Lauri's voice quickened.

Wallace looked at her and smiled a little deeper.

"I think it is a great redistribution of wealth," continued Lauri. "I think it is all orchestrated by the big oil companies and the Federal Reserve and if you ask me they are manipulating this bust to cover their own mistakes..."

"I'm not a stockbroker," said Wallace, interrupting.

Lauri looked down at her hand which had fully clenched his. She slowly tilted her head and looked him directly in the eyes.

"So why are you killing yourself?"

There was silence.

"It's a long story. It's not something that you tell a perfect stranger."

Lauri leaned toward him slowly.

"We wouldn't be perfect strangers if I gave you a little kiss, would we? Wouldn't we be *imperfect* strangers?"

Lauri ever so gently touched her lips to his.

Chapter 2

April 22, 1014
Dublin, Ireland

Ireland had been at war for 200 years, battling kingdoms, invaders, rebels and it was not until Brian Boru emerged as the High King that there was any hope of unity. The last of twelve sons; no one ever thought he would rise to a position of leadership. But as his father and brothers were killed, he rose in the rankings and eventually his cunning ability to hit the enemy and escape into the forests helped him develop a following of his own.

The Vikings were pagans, ruth-less rulers, and they plundered Ireland, burned the churches, stole the lands, massacred the Irish people, enslaved the women and destroyed historical relics.

Hated by Irish countrymen all across the island, the Vikings waged war for decades to crush the Irish.

Brian and his followers were willing to fight the Viking Norsemen even though they were ill-equipped and undermanned. He made up for shortages with his clever tactics, raiding Viking strongholds and luring warriors into the forests where he and his men ambushed them.

In time, his reputation and his army grew and he began uniting Irish clansmen against their enemies. Within a decade, Brian rose to the Crown of Munster, and from there he sought to unite Ireland once and for all. The Vikings were driven out of Southern Ireland but maintained influence in the North.

By the year 1002, Brian successfully united the country, suppressed the

Vikings who remained and ascended to High King. Prosperity followed, but remaining Norsemen still rebelled, and even though King Brian had advanced in years, Vikings in the North formed an allegiance and threw off the rule of his Kingdom.

It was in April of 1014 that King Brian assembled an army near Dublin, the last Viking stronghold.

There, Vikings had brought in reinforcements from neighbors in Scandinavia and Viking boats controlled the sea.

"This battle we are about to wage," said King Brian to men assembled on the eve of April 22, 1014, "will be the final battle! Tomorrow our 6,000 men will drive the Norse from Ireland forever!"

The men cheered in support. It would be a great day if once and for all an end could be put to 200 years of Norse invasions. It would be Christian Irish, civilized and humane, against Viking pagans, foul and vile.

"We will march to victory and we will destroy the Vikings and drive them into the sea!"

Elderly and battle worn from decades of fighting, Brian was an incredible leader. Ever since he was a youth, people listened to him and they died for him. He gave them freedom from those who pillaged Ireland and they passed those victories on to their sons.

Too old to fight in a brutal battle with swords and axes and shields and stones hurled by hand and with slingshots, Brian had passed the duty of leading the men from his home region to his son. An able warrior himself, Murchad led 2,000 men.

As the leaders spoiled for victory and whipped the spirits of the men into a frenzy, a young fighter from the Kingdom of Leinster in central Ireland had his mind elsewhere.

Dubhghall was a handsome man, solid and lean, muscles hardened from years of labor in the fields, skin tanned from exposure, different from most with darker hair and eyes. His parents named him Dubhghall because the name was said to mean "dark stranger."

He had joined the army in its march to Dublin because of his hatred of the Vikings, but he wasn't a warrior. Indeed, he had never been in battle before. He was good at throwing rocks when hunting animals, as were the others in his group--all farm boys encouraged with ideas of victory and notions of liberty.

But Dub's mind was certainly not on the coming battle. Just a mile away was his sweetheart, Meallan, who had agreed to meet him once the others bedded down. Her name meant "lightning" and there was certainly no question that she was properly honored when her parents selected it.

"I told her I would be there once everyone goes to sleep," Dub said to his friend Peadar as they lay resting outside earshot of those preparing for battle.

"You cannot leave now."

"I have to go. I told her I would meet her in the grove by the river."

"We are going into battle tomorrow," said Peadar forcefully.

"Precisely," said Dub, "and I promised her I would see her before the battle." Dub rolled to his side and leaned up on his elbow.

"You need your rest. We all need our rest," argued Peadar.

"I am not weary," Dub said, looking toward embers of a small fire they had built within their camp. Other men sat about or rested, gently talking, too anxious to sleep. It was too dark to do anything except wait for battle. It was the longest wait of a lifetime.

"I am going," announced Dub.

Peadar reached out and grabbed his shoulder.

"You cannot!"

"I will be back before daylight," said Dub.

"It is unwise," said Peadar.

"Then unwise it will be," returned Dub, "I am going to see Meallan."

Dub popped up on to his knees and looked at Peadar.

"I will be back, my friend; do not fear for me."

"God speed," said Peadar as Dub rushed off into the darkness.

A mile away, Meallan crouched at the base of a huge tree. Its sweeping limbs hung out over the water. The moon had risen and there was a glimmer of moonlight dancing in the gentle ripples. She was scared. Just a short distance away were thousands of men ready to do battle. She could be found at any time by a sentry. But, her love for Dub was absolute and her chance to meet him was worth the risk.

Meallan looked around in the darkness. She had pretty eyes and beautiful teeth. Her hair was sandy and in the moonlight it seemed to shine. It was a warm evening but she felt chilled. She was scared, mostly, scared for herself and scared for Dub.

Would he make it? Could he make it? She had already waited for what seemed like an eternity. Maybe she should go. He would not be able to visit her the night before the battle.

He had told her it was the perfect time because everyone would be concentrating on the battle and they would not miss him. But maybe it was impossible to leave the rest of the men.

Meallan felt butterflies in her stomach. Dub was such a wonderful man and she could not ever get him out of her mind. She had thoughts about him all the time, thoughts she didn't know she could have, thoughts that weren't proper for a couple that had not yet married. But she couldn't stop herself. He made her feel wonderful inside and he was all she could talk about and think about and dream about.

There was a crack.

Meallan crouched lower to the base of the tree. She tried not to breathe but she could feel her heart beating out of her chest.

Slowly she scanned the river in front of her, desperately looking for some movement, any movement. Was it him? Was he there? Or was it a soldier? What would they do if they found her? She tried not to breathe but then gasped from holding her breath.

"Psst. Meallan, is that you?"

"Dub?"

"There is no one here," said Dub softly, still in the darkness. "I checked all around."

"Dub?"

Dub stepped over to Meallan, who jumped up and wrapped her arms around him.

"Oh Dub, I was so scared. I was so afraid."

Dub smothered her with arms and body.

"Do not be afraid, Meallan. I'm here now."

"Oh, I love you, Dub. I love you, I do love you."

"We are safe now."

Dub cradled her. She started to relax.

"I am scared, Dub. I am so afraid."

"We are together now, that is

what is important. It is only us here. Nobody else is here."

Dub held her without speaking. Meallan felt his warmth. She slowly relaxed. They scooted down to the ground. Dub leaned against the tree and pulled Meallan up close to him. He could feel her heart beating through her back. Her breathing calmed as he held her from behind.

"I love you, too," he whispered softly.

Meallan reached her right hand over to his left hand to gently caress the back of it with her thumb as he held her. His hands were strong and powerful and rough from work. Hers were sleek and slender, soft and smooth.

"I missed you," she said. "The soldiers have been passing through the village all day. I thought I would see you, but there were so many."

"There are thousands," said Dub. "Many thousands. And King Brian is here!"

Meallan turned toward Dub. "You saw him?"

"No, but he is here. Everyone is talking about it. He will be with us in battle tomorrow. He will be right with us," he said with some excitement.

"Why must you fight?" said Meallan, sadness in her voice. "You are no warrior."

"They have taught me. And besides, I will not be in the heavy fighting. All of us from the farms stay on the sides behind the men with shields and we throw rocks at the other army. We are very good and our rocks disrupt their attention and allow our men to attack."

"It is dangerous," said Meallan, still caressing the back of his hand.

"It is the only way, but it is not like the men who have to fight with their swords. We are far behind them. Even the javelins cannot reach us."

"What if they break through the lines?"

"They will not. King Brian is with us and he has won many battles. Our men will drive the Norse into the sea."

"And you could be killed."

"Why do you say that?"

"I dreamed it," Meallan said softly.

"I will be fine."

"I swear I felt it. I dreamed that something awful would happen to you."

Dub was silent. He moved his hand slightly.

"Touch me," said Meallan distinctly.

Dub lightly kissed the back of Meallan's ear. She leaned toward him.

Meallan picked up his hand with both her hands and placed it on her breast.

"I want you to touch me."

Dub softly cupped his hand. He moved his fingers ever so gently.

"I love you, Dub."

"I love you too."

"You look so young," she said as she gazed at him in the moonlight.

"You make me feel so wonderful," said Dub.

"We will marry," said Meallan. "As soon as the Norse are driven out, we will marry."

"That will be soon. King Brian says we will win tomorrow and that we will have liberty for Ireland."

"Dub, what do you think of the way I look?"

"I love how you look."

"No, you have never seen me. Touch me all over."

Dub squeezed Meallan a little harder and then reached up with his other hand and touched below her breast.

"I want you to love me."

"I do love you," said Dub.

"Love me here, now."

"Meallan, we are not married."

"We will be. You can love me."

Meallan unbuttoned the top of her dress and directed Dub's hand on to her bare skin. She felt his caress as he rubbed slowly and lightly touched her.

"Oh, Dub, I love you so much."

Dub turned her face toward him and kissed the side of her mouth. She responded by turning toward him to kiss him with desire.

When her lips touched his, she felt a tingle she had not known. He kissed her several times slowly and then deeply. His tongue touched hers momentarily.

Meallan felt warmth in her body and she kissed back with her tongue on his lips and against his tongue. Dub rubbed her lightly.

Dub felt his heart beating in his chest as he responded to her with his own physical feelings.

"Touch both my breasts," said Meallan, as she pulled Dub up with her. She pulled open her dress. Dub opened his shirt and the two lovers hugged tightly with their skin touching.

Dub grasped her with his hands and lightly held her. He moved his fingers around to feel all parts of Meallan.

"Lean against me," she said a little louder. As he did, his groin met hers and they felt each other through their clothes.

"Kiss me everywhere."

Dub held his hands in place and kissed one of her breasts. "How?" he whispered.

"Gently," she said.

Dub leaned toward her and lightly bit at her, first one side and then the other. He could hear her breathing and her chest rose and fell a little faster.

Dub removed his hands from Meallan's breasts and said, "I have dreamed about this."

"Feel behind me," said Meallan.

Dub reached down and grasped both sides of her rear. He drew her toward him. She could feel him on both sides of her and wanted him more.

Suddenly he spun her around and with one hand reached up to her breast. With the other, he felt her thighs. She breathed out with pleasure and uttered little sounds that stimulated Dub.

Dub and Meallan formed a union that night, a bond that would go with them forever, a closeness that was so intense as to never be forgotten.

In his arms, Meallan looked up at him.

Look For Me

"My spirit walks in the woods with you," she said.

"I will always be with you."

"*Look for me*," said Dub, "*I will find you.*"

Chapter 3

April 23, 1014
Clontarf, Ireland

For centuries in which man had settled his differences on the battlefield, conflicts began at first light and ended when the night stole away the day. It was that way in 1014 in Central Ireland and so it was during early dawn that six thousand Irishmen prepared to drive almost seven thousand Vikings off their island once and for all.

Near Dublin, the Vikings had taken up a position in a place called Clontarf, where they were fortified and backed up by Viking boats on the sea.

King Brian's army consisted of

formidable warriors in the front, with farmers and countrymen back behind. The Vikings stood shield to shield in a defensive posture to oppose the enemy.

As the armies assembled, leaders marched out into the open space between the two lines and taunted one another and fought individual skirmishes.

Warriors behind cheered as their leaders were victorious.

But the bantering soon gave way to a human conflict matched by none other in battle. Swords clashed, javelins were thrown through the air, battle axes were used to lop off arms and heads. Men from the farms hurled stones through the air at the enemy and used slingshots to place rocks on target.

It was brutal.

The stench of blood and bowels permeated the air in a sickening aroma that only soldiers know.

There were horsemen as well, and they charged and were repelled.

The lines on both sides held for hours as men fell and were replaced from the rear.

The men would battle with all their might, grow tired and retreat to rest and recover.

Dub was a gallant warrior. He had never witnessed such carnage, but he held his ground with his fellow farmers and hurled stones at his targets until his arm was so hot that he thought it would fall off. Again and again and again he would throw stones. Some were accurate and would take out an opposing soldier. Others would miss. But there were plenty of targets and he was ordered to continue and so he did.

Meallan was in the back of his mind the whole day. He couldn't imagine ever being without her and he was anxious for the battle to be won so that he could go to her.

Her love and safety and security was the reason he fought and the reason so many men fell that day. All of them were no doubt there defending a sweetheart or a wife or a mother or a

family. Dub had no idea what others
were thinking. There was no time for
that. He was surprised that he thought
of Meallan at all, but he knew that she
was the reason he had the strength to
go on. Any lesser man would have
slumped from exhaustion, but Dub had
the drive she had given him the night
before and he was determined to save
her from the Norsemen and give her
Irish liberty.

And then he felt it. Out of
nowhere a javelin stabbed into his ab-
domen. He stopped and looked out at
the battlefield. All the noises of metal
clashing disappeared. He saw his
friend Peadar still fighting beside him.
He saw the Viking ships out on the sea.
He saw metal glinting in the afternoon
sunlight. But all he heard was Meallan's voice.

His sweet lover's voice was in his
head. There was pain in his body and
he glanced down to see his hand holding the javelin where it entered his
body and he saw the blood.

"I want you to love me," Meallan's voice repeated in his head, over and over.

Dub tasted blood and his head felt light.

"I do love you," he said. "I do love you. I will always love you. I will love you forever."

The world was in slow motion. There were colors but they ceased to be clear. All the noise was gone and all the pain was gone. Dub was on his knees.

"I want you to love me," he heard one more time.

Then, as his body slowly crumpled to the earth he mouthed the words, *"Look for me. I will find you."*

Peadar didn't see Dub die. He too, was killed seconds later as the Viking men broke through Irish lines and warriors were slashed to pieces.

The Vikings overran that position and slaughtered hundreds of men. But they, too, were tired and the Irish fought them back.

Rumors that the Vikings had fled in their boats was just a ruse and allowed the Vikings to concentrate in one area and break through.

King Brian's son was killed that day too, as were most of the leaders on both sides.

The Irish fought on to nightfall and pushed the remaining Vikings back to the beach where they eventually did try to flee to their boats, only to be met with an incoming high tide. Those in armor who tried to swim, drown. Those who ran out of ground on which to stand, were butchered.

By nightfall, 10,000 men lay dead. By that time it was difficult to distinguish who was whom. The carnage was complete and the air was foul with death.

The Irish were victorious. But the sweetness of victory was quickly lost.

Norsemen who had escaped into the woods stumbled upon King Brian's camp where he was praying to God in thanks for the victory. They killed his bodyguard and quickly beheaded him. The King who had united the country, driven out all invaders and finally set

Ireland free, lay dead on the day of his greatest victory.

It was two days before Meallan's worst fear was realized.

There were not many widows on the battlefield but Meallan searched, hoping beyond hope, that she would find Dub alive.

He wasn't.

When she finally found him, she fell on his body and wailed. How could her man be gone? How could he be one of those who was killed? Why did it have to be him? If only she could have convinced him not to go to battle.

But there he was. Dead. A javelin was through his body. How could this be the same body that had been so loving, that had made her feel so alive? How could this be the man who touched her breasts and had given her pleasures that she had never felt before?

"Look for me," she said. *"I will find you."*

Chapter 4

July 12, 1850
Limerick, Ireland

"May! Look at this, May! We're on our way to America!" Darby Connors made his way past the drying laundry and up a narrow flight of stairs to the small flat he shared with his family. Deep in the slum district of Limerick, Darby was just one of thousands of Irishmen who had left the fields in an effort to survive when crops had failed.

As a young man Darby was hardy and thin, with an abundance of wavy hair and an engaging smile.

"May! Where are you, May?"

He knocked on a door at the top

of the stairs and found it tightly closed. He turned swiftly into his own apartment. No one was there because it was in the middle of the day and everyone was either working or looking for work.

May was his neighbor, and his intended. He expected her to be home with her sister's daughter.

Darby looked out across the alley and spotted May walking with her sister's child.

"May!" shouted Darby. "America!"

May was a beautiful sight. Her long, light hair flowed past her shoulders. She was a small woman, but filled with life and a spirit that could only come from generations of Irish resilience. She had one of the sweetest smiles that had ever been made and a cute little crook to her mouth when she laughed.

"Darby!" she replied.

Darby held up a little flat parcel in his hand. "America! We have passage to America."

May swept up her sister's little

girl and hurried toward Darby. He
clunked down the stairs and rounded
into the alley to meet her. They em-
braced with excitement.

"We're going!" danced Darby.
"We're going to America."

May smiled and laughed with
him, but a concern was evident on her
face. Her huge eyes danced as they
looked into Darby's returning gaze.

"I didn't think it would really
happen," said May.

"Well it has, missy, and now we
can travel to America and get married!"

The two hugged as the little girl
slid down and grasped her aunt's leg.

"Isn't this the most wonderful
news?" asked Darby rhetorically.

He turned toward the broken
down shanties that surrounded him.

"Hey everybody, Darby Connors
is going to America and he's taking May
Carberry with him!"

A grumpy old man's voice came
from nearby, "Ah, shut the hell up."

Darby laughed.

"You'd go yourself if you could,

you old..."

May put her fingers on Darby's lips to quiet him.

"Shhhh," she smiled.

"How about if I come down there and whip your arse, sonny?" said the voice.

Darby pulled May and the little girl toward a closed door below the stairs. He laughed and nodded toward the voice.

He yanked May close to him.

"We are really going this time. It's really going to happen." He kissed May lightly. She responded with a tight squeeze. Darby sensed her tension.

"What's wrong, May?"

May held Darby firmly.

"Are you sure we should go?"

"Of course," said Darby. "It's America."

"But it's so far away and my father has forbidden me to go without being married first."

"There's no time," said Darby. "The *Libenteen* sails in three days. We barely have enough time to gather the provisions. We have to go."

"Maybe we should wait," said May.

"No, we can't wait," said Darby as he released his hug. "Not again."

He held up his parcel of papers.

"This is our passage. For both of us. Master O'Henry has agreed to pay for both of us in exchange for three years labor in America. In Pennsylvania. It's all here."

"But my father..."

"But your father is not ever going to leave Ireland," said Darby. "Your father would rather live like a rat than journey to the one place in the world where a man can live free and own land, and have a family without having to pay rent and taxes."

May grasped Darby and tugged him close.

"It's your dream, not his," she whispered. "He won't allow me to go."

"Then I will marry you right now. We'll go see the priest and he can marry us tomorrow."

"Not without my father's blessing. Father Cantwell would never
allow it."

Darby pulled away and tapped
the wall with his fist. May's niece
buried her head in her aunt's clothing.

"It's America. Why won't he let
us go to America? There is no future for
us here in Ireland. Look around. Look
at the way we live. There's no work.
The farms are all gone. We barely have
enough to eat."

May placed her hand on Darby's
shoulder.

"I know. I know."

That evening, Darby told his
family of the papers for indentured
servitude he had obtained, and they
were pleased that he had finally gotten
them. Darby's brother and father were
happy for him. His mother looked worried.

May's father was angry and once
again forbade her to go to America with
Darby. May cried herself to sleep and
wished that things were different. She

was so confused. She loved Darby and wanted to be his wife, but she had been taught to respect her father's wishes. Why couldn't they get married first, and in time there would be another passage to America?

The morning came quickly. Darby knocked softly on May's door as soon as the family had left to look for work. May stepped out to the landing of the stairs.

"What did your father say?" asked Darby.

"You know what he said," replied May.

"Why does he have to hold us back?" said Darby sternly. "This is not his life, it's ours."

"My father is a good man," said May.

"I know that. But he is not thinking about us. He is thinking about himself."

"He is just trying to protect me," said May.

Darby thumped his chest.

"I'll protect you. If I am to be your husband, then it is my job to protect you."

He hugged May gingerly.

"And," he said softly, "I'll never let anything happen to you."

May snuggled in his arms. She always felt secure when Darby held her.

That evening, Darby asked Mr. Carberry for permission to travel with May to America, and the man angrily denied the request. Darby tried to argue with him, but Mr. Carberry was stern and his mind had been made up. It was not going to happen.

After her family had settled in to sleep, May sneaked out of her flat and met Darby at the base of the stairs.

He grabbed her hand and led her down the alleyway. It was a warm evening and the two hurried through the streets to a small open area they knew. Lovers often found such spots as a way to talk in private, and to get away from the rules that seemed to hinder the youth. There was an intoxicating aroma of blooming summer flowers.

A bit of grass surrounded some old wagon wheels that had been abandoned years before. Darby slowed when they neared their hiding place.

"Let me catch my breath," said May as they sat together in the grass. She giggled.

Darby kissed her quickly and she snapped back playfully.

Darby put his powerful hand to the back of her neck and he pulled her closer.

"Don't you want to kiss a future American?"

May smiled.

"Yes, but what makes you think I would want to kiss you?"

"I guess based upon what happened the last time we were here."

"And what was that?" she probed.

"Well if you can't remember I guess I will have to show you again." Darby leaned toward her. He touched his lips to hers and then retreated. "Does any of this seem familiar?"

"No," said May girlishly. "That's not the way an Irishman kisses." She grabbed Darby and kissed him hard. When she stopped, Darby waved his hand in front of his mouth as if to cool it.

"If that is the way Irishwomen kiss I don't think I want to be an American."

"How do you know American women don't kiss better?" she asked smartly.

"Well I don't know that I do. But I will tell you one thing. The Americans have a lot to learn from the Irish."

Darby kissed May again. Their passion caused the time to fly by. They were unaware of their poverty and of their desperate situation in Ireland. The love between them made it all disappear.

Finally, Darby stopped to look at May.

"You are the most beautiful woman in all the world," he said softly.

May looked at him affection-
ately. A tiny smile crept onto her face.

"Even more beautiful than the
women in America?"

"Especially more beautiful than
the women in America," said Darby.
"That's why I am going to take you
there so that they can see what real
beauty looks like."

May smiled, but slowly, the
smile left her face.

"I can't go to America, Darby.
My father just won't allow it."

"Your father, again," said Darby
with a little anger. "Why does it always
come back to him? Don't you understand that you are to be my bride and
that you can't always do what he
wants?" Darby picked up May's hand.

"We will be married in America.
Our sons will be born Americans. We
will have land and we will have a house
of our own. Don't you see we will never
have that here?"

"I understand Darby, but we can
go the next time. We can get married
with my father's blessing and then we

can go."

Darby released May's hand.

"What if there isn't a next time? What if we never leave Ireland? Do you want to raise your children in these-dregs? Look around you. This is no life for us. There is little work, almost no food."

"We're doing all right," said May.

"Sure we are. Everyone works and we pool our money and have barely enough for the clothes on our backs and the food in our mouths. Your niece doesn't even have shoes. Your sister is out begging. In America they say there are all kinds of jobs for strong Irishmen. We can eventually own land and have a place that nobody will take from us. You don't pay rent to some British nobleman on horseback. You own the land you farm. That will never happen here."

A tear slipped out of May's eye.

"I want to go to America. But not now. Not yet."

Frustrated, Darby turned away from her.

"How can you say that?"

May remained silent.

"I guess I will go to America by myself," said Darby finally.

Those words crushed May and she felt sick to her stomach. Tears dripped out of both her eyes.

"Don't go. Please don't go."

"I have to go, May. I have to do this. A man has to make things better for his family. I can't live like this."

"But this is your home," protested May.

"No," said Darby quietly. "Ireland *was* my home. My home--now--is in America."

The *Libenteen* was set to sail by week's end. Darby was determined not to miss the voyage. He gathered his provisions, required for as much as a ten week trip, and packed them in a trunk that he could barely haul.

The list provided by the shipping company was specific:

70 pounds hard bread

8 pounds butter
24 pounds meat
10 pounds sidepork
1 small keg of herring
8/3 tonne potatoes
20 pounds rye and barley flour
½ bushel dried peas
½ bushel pearl barley
3 pounds coffee
3 pounds sugar
2½ pounds syrup
Quantities of salt, pepper, vinegar and onions

He would be given three quarts of water each day and firewood by the ship's crew and he was expected to provide his own utensils and bedding. It was a lot to gather and Darby only had his brother to help.

May tried to dissuade Darby from going, but his mind was made up. The day before departure, May didn't even speak to him.

With provisions set and ready the night before, Darby looked for May but could not find her. He figured her father was hiding her and so he re-signed himself to giving her a letter. He couldn't write and she couldn't read, so he had a man near the center of town write the letter for him.

My dearest May. You know that this trip is important to me, to us. I cannot miss the opportunity to go to America again. If we do not go now, we may never go. I understand your respect for your father and so I will not ask you again.

I will go ahead of you and establish myself in America. I will leave word with the shipping company where I have gone and as soon as I can arrange for passage I will send for you. My brother will also try to come to America and he can escort you when you feel the time is right.

As for me, I cannot wait. You know that about me. You know that this is the best thing for us. I love you dearly and will love you with all my heart forever. Come to America and look for me. I will be there to find you.

Your future husband, Darby.

Darby folded the letter and gave it to his brother with instructions to personally hand it to May, and it was agreed.

As the sun rose, the 312 passengers who were to board the sailing ship *Libenteen* gathered on the dock in Limerick. The ship's crew was busy getting the vessel ready to get underway. One by one, the passengers showed their papers and had their provisions taken from them by men who would stack them in the ship's hold or rope them down in the aisles. The passengers gathered on the deck and awaited assignments below.

The sun was shining brightly and it looked like there would be good winds by the time the ship was ready to cast off.

Darby hugged his mother. He said goodbye to his father and brother.

"You'll remember the note, little brother," said Darby.

"Does an Irishman ever forget?"

his brother replied.

"I will say this," replied Darby, "I will sail back to Ireland and lay in to you with a fistful of anger if you do."

"Don't worry. I will see that it is done."

Darby made his way up the gangplank on to the ship's deck. His name was called and he was ushered to the back of the ship and told to wait.

There was such a buzz of activity that he thought he would drop dead of excitement. His heart longed for May, but this was what he had to do to change his world. And all around him were hundreds more immigrants who were dreaming of better lives in America.

Before long, he was taken down to the "tweendeck" as they called it, and assigned to a bunk.

It was dark on the middeck, and crowded. There were lines and lines of bunks, two high, each made to sleep four passengers. The ceiling was scarcely six feet from the floor. Below the rough wooden floor was the ship's hold where a steady stream of men carried passengers' provisions. They were stacked in on top of the cargo like cordwood.

Darby looked at the ladder that led below. The kerosene lamps danced and created a strange glow. He wondered how he was going to find his provisions once it was time to sail, and how in the world it would all be sorted out once they were at sea.

On his assigned bunk he placed his bedding-- a pillow and blanket. He had been advised to bring an animal skin for warmth but he didn't have one. He judged that he could sleep in his clothes and his blanket was warm. Besides, it was summer and he figured it couldn't get too cold at sea.

As Darby looked about, he heard the sails being rigged, so he made his way back up the steep ladder through the wooden hatch. The deck was crowded with passengers--referred to by the crew as steerage.

Darby wondered if that was a

reference to steers as he began to feel a little bit like livestock himself.

The captain shouted some orders. Crew members snapped into action. The ropes were cast off and the ship began to move away from the dock.

Family members on land waved at their loved ones.

"Goodbye Momma! Goodbye Father!" said Darby.

He spotted his brother running along the ship as it pulled away faster and faster.

"You won't forget?"

His brother patted his chest. "I will not forget my brother Darby, I will find your sweetheart for you!"

As exciting as it was to depart, Darby's heart felt as though it would explode. Would he ever see May again? Would he ever see his mother and father again? Would he ever see his brother again?

With the other passengers, Darby stared back at Ireland until it had disappeared into the ocean. He watched as it got smaller and smaller and then was nothing.

How strange, he thought, that it was still there, the place where he was born and spent his whole life, but he could no longer see it.

It gave him an anxious feeling and a sense of loss that he couldn't describe.

Ireland was gone. May was gone. Sweet May. She was the most lovely girl in the world.

Darby turned and looked toward the front of the ship. The huge sails billowed with wind as the ship cut through the water. There were seagulls visible from time to time, but nothing else. There was only water.

As the sun began to set, Darby made his way down to the hatch that led to his bunk. There were passengers streaming toward their areas and so Darby had to wait his turn.

But just before he stepped onto the ladder he felt a hand tug at his arm. He had been bumped by people all day, so didn't expect anything different until he heard his name.

"Darby."

He reeled around and saw something he couldn't believe. It was May!

She grabbed him.

"May, what are you doing here?"

"Darby," May replied.

Darby kissed her neck as he held her.

"Why?"

"Let's just say I didn't want to go down in history as the girl who broke your heart."

Darby squeezed her and kissed her.

"But how?"

"It doesn't matter. What matters is that I'm here with you."

"But what about your father?"

"He knows," said May. "He knows I wouldn't let you go without me."

"And how did you get on the ship?"

"That was a little tricky. I convinced the girl who was loading the captain's cookware, that the company had hired me to help. I just never got off the ship."

Darby looked around carefully.

"Stowaway?" he whispered.

"How are they going to know? You think they keep track of the steerage? Everybody knows that once you are on board they don't call names."

Darby smiled.

"I'm beginning to think you are evil."

"Why?"

"Because you get what you want, no matter what," he said.

"Doesn't that just make me an American?"

Darby smiled. "I suppose it does."

The two walked over to the railing of the ship and looked out over the ocean. The sun set in earnest. The sky glowed red with long beams of light streaming over the clouds. The smell of saltwater was in the air as the ship clipped through the water and a slight spray flipped up onto the deck.

"All steerage below," called out

one of the crew members.

Darby kissed May.

"You are the love of my life," he whispered.

Below the deck the lamps had been lit, but the light was poor. Darby pulled May down the center aisle in search of his bunk. Finally, he found it. There were three men already in the bunk when he arrived.

The bunks were made for four, but families did sleep together and occasionally there were five or six in a bunk.

Darby approached the bunk.

"This is mine here," he said to an older Irishman by the name of Henry who was taking up most of the available space and encroaching on Darby's bedding.

"You two comin' in here?" Henry asked.

"Yes, yes, that's for us right there," said Darby.

"Oh, laddie, this bunk is not big enough for all of us," said Henry.

"Well it is just going to have to be," said Darby as he bumped his head on the upper bunk while he was leaning in toward his.

May smiled.

"Those wankers," replied Henry. "How do they expect a man to sleep with another man's wife in the same bunk?"

"Well, she's ah, well," Darby puffed up. "You stay away from my wife."

"No offense intended laddie," said Henry, "It's just the way they treat the Irish."

"That's right," said Darby. "The Irish are lower than the Scots."

A couple of others in the area who were listening in chuckled.

"Hear, hear," someone said.

"But at least there aren't any British on board," someone else cracked. That caused a good laugh. "They're too scared to go to America lest the Yankees powder their arse again!"

That caused full out laughter and all of a sudden somebody played a tune on a pennywhistle.

"I hope he can play," said another, "or this will be a long trip."
There was more laughter.

The pennywhistler kept tooting
and the Irish steerage recognized his
song.

We are the Irish,
We work the whole day through,
We are the Irish,
And the British are fools.

We are the Irish,
We plow the fields of crops,
We are the Irish,
And the Brits are only cops.

We are the Irish,
We lay down in meadows so sparse,
We are the Irish,
And the King of England can kiss our
arse!

We are the Irish!
And the King can kiss our arse!
We are the Irish!

And the King of England can kiss our arse!

In time, the hatch above was slammed shut and a sailor above shouted.

"Lights out! Captain's orders!"

The song went another chorus:

We are the Irish!
And the King can kiss our arse!
We are the Irish!
And the *Libenteen* Captain can kiss our arse!

Amid laughter the kerosene lamps were quickly snuffed out.

"All quiet now," said the sailor.

"And you can kiss my arse," said an Irishman in the darkness.

There was muffled laughter.

It was going to be a tough journey, for sure, but the Irish spirit would make it tolerable. Song and music could take the place of weary feelings.

May snuggled in Darby's arms. There wasn't enough room in the bunk, so she placed her head on his chest and got as close to him as she could.

"I can't believe you're here," Darby whispered.

"I wouldn't have missed being with you for anything," she replied.

"Okay mate," said Henry, "so you're both happy to be here. Now get some shuteye."

"Good night then," said Darby softly. And then aloud, "Good night everybody!"

"Only an Irishman would call it a good night on a tiny sailing ship in the middle of the ocean with a bunch of Irishmen," said a voice in the darkness.

There were chuckles.

"Shut up, Horace," came a voice in the darkness, followed by a thump as his wife hit his chest.

Chapter 5

July 16, 1850
Atlantic Ocean

Ship's rules required that all steerage passengers be out of bed and dressed by 7 o'clock am. With just two toilets in each section, one at either end, the lines were long and the wait was sometimes unbearable. Women and children were allowed to go first.

On the main deck above, a small kitchen shanty was available for passengers to heat coffee or make porridge. Ship's crew members rationed water and firewood for passenger use.

The kitchen shanty was a small enclosure with a floor made from a deep layer of sand. Inside, women crouched to build open fires to make breakfast. As the ship tossed back and forth on the swell of the ocean, pots often spilled and the ladies had to constantly keep hold of them to prevent losing precious provisions.

Even though the shanty did have a smokestack, when the ship was underway, the smoke was prevented from exiting the stack by the air pressure of the sailing vessel. This caused smoke to build up inside the shanty and torture the cooks.

It was not uncommon for women to hurry out of the shanty in order to breathe fresh air or dry tearing eyes. It was so crowded that when a woman went outside to rub her eyes and catch her breath, another woman would quickly take her place. Then, upon returning, the first woman would find her firewood being used and her pot sitting off in the sand.

Even the most shy of the women would find themselves arguing over their place, their wood and how long it takes to boil a pot of water. Allegiances formed, though, and women found themselves sticking together and looking out for one another in opposition to those who were a bit more pushy.

May was such a quiet girl that she found herself losing her place often and considered the cooking ordeal to be quite enough for the Irish spirit of any emigrant.

Darby couldn't believe the mess in the hold. Down below the 'tween-deck' were not only the passengers' trunks and provisions, but the ship's cargo. The area was stacked to the ceiling and jammed so tight that it was impossible to get anything without moving everything.

"Who in their right faculties loaded this ship?" asked Darby with irritation as two other men helped him try to find specific trunks.

"They have cargo on top of provisions and provisions at the bottom of everything. Where are we supposed to stack something to get at something else?"

"Just keep movin' 'em laddie, we'll break this puzzle yet," said Eli, a middle-aged man with flame red hair.

Sweat poured down Darby's face.

"They must have brought the British on this ship to supervise the loading."

"Hand me that one there," said Eli. "Put 'er up on the 'tweendeck' and we'll make ourselves a hole."

Darby struggled to unwedge a trunk. Most of the baggage was too heavy for one man but he grunted and used as much leverage as he could muster to drag one trunk across another. Hands reached down from above and hoisted it out of the way.

"That'll do 'er," said Eli with a smile. "Now anudder."

Together, the men were able to pull a series of trunks out of the hold and stack them above. As they made a space, they moved the ship's cargo to the bottom and stacked the passenger trunks on top.

"You might have thought somebody in the captain's employ would have thought of this while we were at the dock," said Darby as the ship rocked from side to side and trunks that had previously been stacked, shifted.

"Hand 'er some line down here," shouted Eli.

Instantly a hand held a coil of rope through the opening in the ceiling.

In time, the men were able to re-organize the load. They tied off what they could and made an effort to mark the trunks so that each day it would be easier to get to the food as it was needed.

From above, there was the smell of cured mutton and soft whey cheese as various passengers got to their trunks and removed the day's portions.

Darby's body was aching, but he kept working until the job was done.

Finally, he and the others climbed out of the hold, to the middeck and on up to the main deck to get some air.

The cool salt air felt good on Darby's sweaty body. It was summer and it had gotten quite hot below with little ventilation and not much room to move.

Darby looked out over the ocean. All he could see was water. Then, he turned his attention to the cooking shanty where he spotted May sitting with her head down.

He jumped over an older couple resting against a railing and went to her.

"May, are you all right?"

May looked up at him with tears in her reddened eyes. The smoke had driven her out of the cooking shanty time and time again. The whole time Darby was rearranging cargo and trunks, she couldn't even boil a pot of water. Most of it had spilled on the sand in the shack.

May held the pot up to Darby so he could see there was barely any left.

"Coffee?" asked Darby.

May bowed her head.

Darby grabbed the pot and held it up. He stood and showed it around.

"Irish coffee, anyone? The lady

here has had a wee bit a trouble making it warm, but then, it seems it is way too crowded on this fine ship for a fair young lass to get up to the fire.

"I'll tell you what, strangers. Let us be friends and share our coffee this morning. Does anyone want a taste of ours?"

A couple of passengers seemed amused and one man reached over and poured some of his coffee into Darby's pot.

"Thank you very much, sir. I can see you're a fine man from Ireland on your way to earn your fortune in America."

May looked up and marveled how Darby could turn such a situation around.

"Anyone else to share in this man's fortune?"

Another man poured a little coffee into Darby's pot. Then a woman added more.

"That's it! Our cup runneth over. God tells us that the meek shall inherit the earth and I am here to tell you that you all shall be the kings and queens of Pennsylvania!"

"Hear, hear," said one man.

"Then we have solved our problem in the Irish way and may the blessings of the Lord rain down upon you because of your noble generosity."

A couple of the passengers laughed as Darby knelt beside May and offered her the warm pot of coffee. She gazed at him with affection, took the pot and sipped from it.

Darby was that kind of man. Poor as the dirt below his feet when he farmed back in Ireland, but hard working and clever. Nothing could daunt his spirit and when things were not going his way, he had a way about him. May loved him for that. Darby was a man who could change destiny, who could make even the worst situation better. Where he got that spirit she did not know, but she was sure of one thing. He had a different type of soul; an old soul.

Life on board the *Libenteen* was

a challenge every single day. There were just way too many passengers and as long as sailing was good, it didn't seem so bad. May and Darby wandered the deck, listened to Irish song, even danced occasionally. They could look out over the deep blue sea and dream of America and dream of their life together. Darby was full of ideas. After paying off his indentured servitude his plan was to acquire property and start a small farm of his own, build a house, have children and really become an American.

May was so glad to be with him. She missed her family at home, but she knew that even at the age of 17, it was overdue for her to marry and give Darby the son he said he'd have.

The food was mostly bad on board the ship. All the passengers were responsible for their own provisions and while some took the instructions of the shipping company literally, others had way too much of some things and not enough of others. There was a lot of trading and it generally worked out.

Darby and May did not have enough food. When May sneaked on to the ship, she did not bring provisions aboard, so Darby shared his with her. But two people eating the food for one was not enough. May was not a big girl to start, but as the weeks wore on she lost weight. Occasionally another passenger keen to the situation would offer a little something in a kind gesture. May would politely refuse but then thank them and eat it anyway.

In bad seas, life aboard the sailing vessel was unbearable. It was impossible to stay up on deck because of the crashing waves, and steerage was ordered below and the hatches were closed.

If the hatches remained open, sea water would splash in and run to the hold and stay. Even with precautions, water still got in and had to be painstakingly bailed.

When the hatches were battened down, the middeck was dark and the ventilation was poor. In especially rough waters, even the kerosene lamps could not be used for fear of falling and starting a fire.

As the ship tossed on the seas, passengers became seasick and the smell of vomit made others sick as well.

Dysentery was common, and when a storm would not let up for days the stench got so bad as to threaten the health of the other passengers.

Occasionally a crew member would work his way below with burning tar. The tar was a bad smell, but it helped clean the air and was not as putrid as days of human waste and vomit.

The conditions below were so horrific that at times someone would scream out in frustration and he would have to be restrained by those around him.

May was sick. She stayed sick for days and vomited and had so much diarrhea that there was nothing left inside her. Darby tried to comfort her. He used rationed water to wipe her forehead. She lay in the bunk and he crouched beside her.

"Darby, I want to go home," she whispered weakly.

"We'll get there," said Darby.

"How much longer?"

"Captain says two weeks, maybe three."

"What about this storm? When is it going to be over?"

"He doesn't know. Said he's seen them last for more than a week."

"I can't do this," said May. "I can't do this anymore."

Darby rubbed her head. Her eyes were sunken and dark. He prayed for her and asked God to stop the storm and help the passengers.

That made May feel better but she was still so weak that she could barely lift up her head. She looked over at Darby with affection. This man beside her would do anything for her. He would protect her and keep her and love her. He would fight for her and work so that she had a better life. He was an amazing man.

"I love you," she whispered almost silently.

Lost in his own thoughts, Darby didn't hear her. He held her hand and felt her, but as the night wore on and the waves tossed about the ship, he was not sure when May took her last breath. All he knew for sure is that sometime that night she did. She in the bed, he crouched on the floor beside her, the greatest love of a lifetime was taken from him.

Lightning struck the ship during the night, and cracked one of the yardarms. The rain put out the fire, but crew had to climb the mast to secure the sail.

In the morning, it took both Henry and Eli to separate Darby from May's body. He was angry and alone and so distraught that the other passengers did everything they could to comfort him. This strong man was brought to his knees, his heart ripped out, his insides torn to pieces, his head dizzy with grief.

The ship's carpenter built a casket from rough-hewn timber he had on board. He carefully drilled holes in the sides. Sand was put in the bottom to give the coffin weight.

With reverence, May's body was wrapped in bedding and securely tied.

The storm broke two days later and the Captain assembled the passengers and crew on deck.

With Darby standing between Henry and Eli, the Captain blessed May's body, blessed Darby and ordered the coffin placed over the side.

The holes were to allow water in so that the coffin would sink, but as the people watched the wooden raft with May's remains in it, it did not sink right away. The ship continued its trek forward. Darby and others stood at the rail and watched the coffin until it was out of sight. The only sound was that of the sails and the water lapping on the sides of the ship.

It was then that Darby broke down and cried from his gut. He grasped the railing and shouted out, "*Look for me,* May! *I will find you!*"

Chapter 6

September 8, 1850
America

The *Libenteen* made it into New York Harbor two weeks later. Once the storm broke, the winds were favorable and the trip ended quickly. Darby had said little since May died, and while all were on deck to see land, Darby's heart was lacking the joy it once had. As New York Harbor came into sight, Darby's chest pounded. He could smell fresh air.

"We're here May. Sweet May," he said softly.

Arriving in America was his dream. But without May it would always be a broken dream.

There were huge lines on shore, piles of cargo and passenger trunks; Americans processing immigrants; questions, confusion and uncertainty.

For Darby, it was bittersweet. He wanted to be in America, but not like this. The loneliness was crushing and he found himself in a crippling daze.

The Irish community welcomed him and the others, and helped their former countrymen find housing and look for jobs.

Jobs were scarce. Often job notices ended with *Irish Need Not Apply*.

There were just too many immigrants in New York and so as he had agreed to do for Master O'Henry who had paid his passage, Darby set off walking for Pennsylvania.

There, he had heard there would be work and once he fulfilled his obligation of three years labor to Master O'Henry, he'd be free to start his own life.

But what kind of life would it be without May? How could he ever be happy again? It was so different without her as part of his dream.

Darby walked the 120 miles to Scranton. It was an enjoyable journey, beautiful rolling hills by day, star-filled nights in darkness. He slept along the road where many others had traveled ahead of him. He had a little food left from the transatlantic crossing, mainly flatbread and butter. He had been lucky and sold his trunk in New York, but the money would not last.

He wasn't sure where he was going except Scranton. O'Henry had an address in the packet that contained passage on the ship but Darby had no idea where that was, other than Scranton.

He figured when he arrived someone would help him.

It was pretty amazing, Darby thought, that a man he had never met trusted him to travel all the way from Ireland and show up for three years labor. But as it happened, there were others on the same road with similar papers--indentured servants--willing to work to get to America.

When Darby arrived in Scranton, he did not find it difficult to locate Master O'Henry. It seemed O'Henry & Sons was a well-known construction firm and hundreds of Irish were in his employ.

Darby never did meet Master O'Henry, or any of the sons. He was simply registered and given instructions where he would sleep the night. The next day he'd be shipped out on the railroad where he would find himself to be a railroad worker.

From farm to railroad, thought Darby, this America is already looking to be the land of opportunity!

By day, Darby handled huge timbers. There were two men on each railroad tie, placed on the ground one after the other, steel rails dropped in place by twenty men, pounded in place with sledge hammers. By night, he slept in a camp with a hundred other men, food served, fires built, conversation and dreams shared openly.

It was a good life for Darby, and the three years passed quickly. He longed for May, but there wasn't anything he could do but put his mind into his work.

It was a great day when he was handed his release from O'Henry & Sons and offered a job. He was free to go but he was welcome to stay. But now, instead of just food he would be offered wages as well.

Darby stayed.

Chapter 7

1871
Pennsylvania

Somehow another 17 years passed. The Civil War came and went. Lincoln was shot and the country mourned and then rebuilt.

Darby was good with people, so he worked his way up to being in charge of one of the O'Henry construction crews. His work took him across America building a frenzy of railroad lines. He became strong and resolute. He saw men die, and he held them as they spit blood from being crushed by trellis crossing timbers. He witnessed a man plummet to his death.

The Irish built the rail lines that

O'Henry designed and the Irish suffered the hardships of cold nights, hot days, rain and mud; blistering heat.

By 1871, Darby had built enough rail to cross the country and was tired of that life. He was tired of living out of a tent and a wagon. Long gone was the idea of being a farmer, though he had saved some money and was thinking he could get work in Scranton and settle down. May was never far from his mind and many a railroad tie had her name carved on them. He never told anyone about May, lied and said he carved "May" because that was his favorite month. He missed her terribly and missed the idea of being with her. His American dream was mighty, but it was not the same without the sweet girl of his dreams. A new nation was being forged and he was part of it. But he still had an emptiness inside that nothing could fill. He felt as though his soul was lonely and only the work numbed him to the reality of having lost her.

Steam engines ran on coal and

the one thing Pennsylvania had was coal, so Darby moved back to Scranton and determined that he'd become a miner and live in a permanent place near the mine.

Unlike some workers, Darby was older, 40 by then, and he had money saved. He did not have to live in a mine town, so he found a place in Scranton not far from a railroad he had helped build twenty years before. It was a small apartment, owned by a kind land-lord, just a short distance from the train he would need to take to the mining camp.

Work notices for coal mines were plentiful. Anthracite was in demand, but the work was tricky. Seams of coal did not run continously, but sometimes would zig and zag and play out and then pick up again a few dozen feet lower or higher depending upon how the earth twisted it all together. It took a special sense and strong desire to mine anthracite. The idea of extract-ing coal from the ground appealed to Darby somehow. It was the challenge, and the ingenuity that it required, that attracted him.

On a Spring day in 1871, Darby made his way to the Pittsburgh Mining Company, Limited, from which he had found a notice someone had told him was seeking foremen. The mine was just outside Scranton so the train journey was quick.

A long string of men led from the train station up the road into the hills. It wasn't a great distance, but it was pretty steep, so Darby caught himself breathing a little deeper, having to catch his breath to talk with the men headed in the same direction.

There were jobs for sure, they told him. The work in the mine was unending and a good railroad man and his skill with timbers was always appreciated.

At the top of the hill stood a clapboard building that had been painted red when it was new, but had faded over the years to a crimson brown. The road was black from hauling coal down the slopes. It was a little chilly in the hills and Darby noticed that he could see his breath as he puffed up the steep grade. Rays of sunlight peeked between two mountains on the horizon. He passed a corral of mules that were used to work the coal.

Off in the distance were the tell-tale signs of a mine--tall structures for handling hoists, rusted tin shacks, steel mine cars, railroad tracks, a huge breaker building, and men, there were a lot of men.

Darby found a bevy of workers standing in a line at a doorway he was told was the office. They were all looking for jobs, some young, others a bit older, but no one as advanced in years as he.

Darby tried to make small talk, but he found himself distracted. Maybe quitting the railroad wasn't such a good idea after all. There, he was in charge. There, he was the one interviewing potential laborers. There, he had a respected position.

So lost in thoughts he was that he did not even hear the young woman from inside call, "Next" when it was his turn to go inside. A man beside him poked him. "You gonna go?"

"Yes, sure," said Darby, "I didn't come all the way up here for nothing."

Darby stepped into the building. His heavy boots pounded the wooden floor and bits of mud tracked behind him. He stepped toward a long, wooden table. It was covered with paper, applications most likely, and there were a couple of other men sitting in the room, writing. Two or three of them were talking.

"Sir," said Mary Hillten, as she extended a form toward Darby, "you're going to need to fill this out first."

Darby caught the woman's eyes. She saw him holding the glance ever so slightly. He could see a gentle peace in her ice blue eyes. She had a stunning beauty that took his breath away.

"Sir?" said Mary, "you need to..."

"I'm sorry," said Darby interrupting.

"That's all right," she replied, "this application needs to be filled out."

Darby looked at her eyes a moment longer. There was a bit of a silence.

"Do you need a pencil?"

"Sure," said Darby.

A small smile made its way onto Mary's face. She noticed that he noticed. Men looked at her all the time, but this was different. He was older than most who came in looking for work, with a rough handsomeness that comes from a man who had used his back to work but was fully capable of using his mind.

When Darby took the pencil from her, their hands touched ever so quickly. It was a bit of a fumble on Darby's part. He was so enthralled at looking at her eyes that he misjudged the distance to her hand.

"I'm sorry," he said as he turned, "where?"

"Just sit anywhere you can find a place."

Darby looked around the office. There was one vacant chair, but he decided to step outside anyway.

As he walked through the doorway he heard Mary call out again, "Next."

As he sat outside, he wondered about her. What a beautiful girl to be working among all these rough, dirty men. She must be related to the owner, probably the owner's daughter or a relative of some kind.

Darby smiled to himself. Inside he felt good. It was good to be applying for work, and it was good to be seeking work from the company that hired that girl.

The application was just one page, but Darby had a problem. He had worked for O'Henry for years, had led men across the prairie, had been responsible for hundreds of dollars worth of payroll. But despite that, Darby still couldn't read. He never learned how. He didn't have the time or the need, or maybe it was both.

He had always worked for O'Henry and had never filled out a job application before.

Darby looked up from the corner of the front deck where he was sitting next to the stairs. There was a steady line of men applying for jobs. Surely they could read and the ones that couldn't, weren't too proud to ask for help. But they were younger, some just in from Ireland.

A couple of minutes passed as Darby considered his predicament. Would they hire him and put him in a supervisory position if he couldn't read? What if they hired him and found out later that he was a worker without any schooling?

Then there was a tap on his shoulder. Darby saw a pair of feet beside him.

"Sir?" asked Mary, as she stood over him.

Darby looked up, a little startled. "Yes?"

"Do you need some help with that?"

Darby's mind flashed without an answer. He pointed at the document.

"No, I was just thinking about my answers."

Mary smiled. She had seen that response before.

"Well, after you think about them awhile, why don't you let me help you?"

"I can get it," said Darby, trying to hide his secret.

Mary smiled and put her hands on her hips. Darby looked at how beautifully shaped she was.

"I'll be fine," he reiterated.

"Suit yourself." Mary turned toward the line of men coming up the stairs. "We're hiring for all mining positions," she said. "Miners, nippers, driver boys. Applications are at the head of this line. If you cannot read the application we will help you fill it out."

Darby watched in amazement how this young woman took charge.

She turned toward Darby, who pretended to be starting to fill out the application.

"Sir, can I help you with that? I've filled out hundreds of these and I can ask you all the questions by heart."

Darby grinned at her. "That would be very nice."

"C'mon," she said, "we've got an open table inside."

Darby followed her back into the office where he noticed that an older man had taken her place handing out applications. He looked strict and had a meanness about him. He hunched over the table where the top of his thinning hair could be seen.

"Have a seat right here," directed Mary as she sat down across the corner of the table.

"Can you write at all?"

"No," said Darby softly, embarrassed.

"That's quite all right. There are no books in the mine, unless you're the fire boss and we're not really hiring those. But I think I'll need that pencil more than you will."

Darby smiled and handed it over to her.

"First question, what is your name?"

"Darby Connors."

"Is that with an 'e' or an 'o' at the end?" asked Mary.

"What?" said Darby.

"Connors. Is it Connors or Conners?"

"O," said Darby.

"Date of birth?"

"Shouldn't I know your name first?" asked Darby.

Mary smiled. "I already have a job."

"But what should I call you?"

"You know how many times I get that every day?"

"Well today's a new day."

Mary's tongue touched her lip slightly as she hesitated.

"So what kind of answer do you give when people ask you a question like that?" insisted Darby.

Mary laughed slightly under her breath.

"You're pretty persistent, Mr. Connors."

"Well that's how I get what I want and I really want a job here."

"You know you're older than most of these men here. This is hard labor."

"Really? I thought that coal just dug itself out of the ground and jumped in those rail cars and the mules just hauled it to the cage without asking them.

"You know, ma'am, whatever your name is, I built the railroad that runs up to this mine. And I didn't do it with my back. I did it with my head. Steel rails and timber are pretty heavy on a man's back after 17 years so he learns how to use a block and tackle and let the weight of the object you're setting in place help you move it."

"Mary."

Darby held his hand out toward Mary. She shook it.

"Pleased to meet you Mary, Mary of the Pittsburgh Mining Company, Limited in Scranton, Pennsylvania."

"No, Mary is just fine," responded Mary with a little giggle.

"Now there is a question you are going to have to answer for me if I am going to be an inside boss at this mine..."

Mary laughed a little at how sure he was about the job.

"Why in the world would a mining company located in Scranton, Pennsylvania be called the Pittsburgh Mining Company, Limited, when we aren't anywhere close to Pittsburgh? It seems like it should be the Scranton Mining Company, Limited."

A big smile had taken over Mary's face.

"I guess that's just the way the owner wanted it."

"Say it isn't so, lass," said Darby, "even in America things don't always make sense."

"How about that date of birth, now?"

Darby liked this girl, this Mary whoever she was. She was fun to joke with and he could see she was entertained by his antics.

He watched her carefully as she

filled out the employment form. Her hands were sleek and pretty and her handwriting was proper and neat. He judged that she was maybe twenty years old, if that, probably the daughter of somebody for sure, somebody who had an interest in the mine or ran the place.

It didn't take long for the management of the Pittsburgh Mining Company, Ltd. to make a decision about hiring Darby. They liked him because of his railroad experience and there was one thing for sure about coal mining-- somebody had to know what they were doing when it came to building tunnels for the gangways and reinforcing them with timbers. Darby had been told to wait and by day's end, Mary assembled a large collection of men at the office and read off a list of names. Almost everyone was hired. A few were not, mostly blacks and people who the mining company just didn't feel like hiring.

Darby's name was called and he was told that he would be going to work as an assistant to an inside boss. The pay was not as good as he had been used to at the railroad, but it was reasonable, given that he had no mining experience at all. He could not earn the best wage as the seasoned miners did.

But that was okay. In time, Darby would work his way up, he always did.

Three weeks passed before Darby saw Mary again. He had hoped he would run across her and always looked toward the office when he made his way to work and then again when he left at the end of the shift. When he finally did see her, it was pleasant for him because he was beginning to wonder if she had only worked there when they were hiring so many men.

The mine had taken on new contracts and had decided to dig new tunnels to increase production, and as it happened Darby's application was timed perfectly. They were even building a new shaft to reach a seam they believed was 750 feet below the surface.

In three weeks, Darby gained the respect of his inside boss, a man named John Julias, and the men started looking up to him. He certainly knew how to move timber and fasten it together.

As he told them, if he could build bridges across ravines and steam steel engines across them, he could build tunnel structures that would hold up mountains.

When he saw Mary, Darby waved and said, "Hello."

She did not respond. Maybe she didn't see him. But she did not look happy and Darby thought that she might have been crying. She was at the office, standing outside on the porch.

Darby thought about stopping to speak to her, but he would have had to climb a long flight of stairs and without some business with the office, saying something just to her might have been considered improper.

As he walked down the hill toward the train to take him back into town, he wondered about Mary. She was such a pretty girl. What was it that was upsetting her? Should he have stopped and said something? What would be so wrong with reaching out to her to comfort her in time of need?

The next day was a bad day for the Pittsburgh Mining Company, Limited. Darby had heard about it on the way to work on the train. The roof in one of the gangways where men walked and mules towed carts of coal had collapsed. Men were trapped, probably some dead.

Darby's first hope was that no one was hurt and his second was that the collapse was not in his area.

When Darby arrived at the station, there were men everywhere. It seemed as though every miner, regardless of shift, was at the station or headed up the hill. With gear clanging and "hurry ups" shouted, Darby pushed up the steep grade with all his might.

On the way up, he heard that the collapse was in No. 32, one of the older seams and that there was no word about survivors.

There were crews being assembled and men were already down below digging furiously to uncover and remove as much debris as possible. The hoist above was running the gunboat up and down continuously, one whistle to raise it and go, two to lower it. Men were all over the wood bonnet keeping the hoist engine running, watching for overheating, getting the maximum out of the machinery.

It was dangerous work below because one collapse can always trigger another, and the gangway was dark with coal dust. Darby's assignment was to keep debris moving, get it out of the mine as fast as possible and dumped away from the entrance. Men were sent in to dig with pick and axe for fifteen minutes and then they were relieved. What they dug, others shoveled into the small mule-drawn rail cars. These were whisked outside and crews emptied them and sent them back in for refilling. Three whistles meant that men were in the cage being hoisted down to relieve those sweating below.

Good progress was made that first day, but there was a long way to go. The mine was always wet, but No. 32 was particularly sloppy. It was tough work.

Heads were counted and it was determined that 35 men were trapped by the cave-in. Their names were carefully picked off a large pegboard that showed by brass button who was in and who was out.

John Julias was in the mine when the roof caved in. That news surprised Darby because Julias had worked the last shift with him the day before and he was not due to come back on until later.

"They say Julias was in the mine?" Darby asked as a line supervisor passed his rolling cart.

"Yeah, he was."

"What was he doing in there?" asked Darby. There was no answer.

The trouble with a cave-in is the lack of oxygen. Anthracite seams can run miles into the side of a mountain.

There is no way to locate the room from outside, much less any hope of drilling into it with equipment from above. If you are going to get the men out, you have to dig them out, by hand, and quickly. It was muddy work. The oxygen inside will last for awhile, but depending upon how many men and how deep they were in the tunnel, it could be days or just hours.

Mining accidents were common in the 1870s, but nobody ever liked them. The mining bosses hated them because production stopped. The miners hated them because their colleagues often perished.

Darby had seen death before, on the railroad. But the prospect of 35 men dying all at once in a single accident filled him with anguish. He had just gotten to know some of these men, and Julias had become a friend. It would be tough to lose any of them.

Nightfall didn't stop the miners. Darby was told to rest with his crew and new crews were brought on. The rule was that everybody digs and rests, digs and rests, digs and rests until the job is done. It could go on for many hours.

"What do you think happened?" Darby asked one of the old timers.

"Same thing as always happens."

"What's that?"

"Timber gives way, roof caves in. Not enough timber in most of these gangways. All these roofs are pressin'," said the bearded miner as he pointed out across the hills. "Too big a hurry to get that coal out of there." His face covered with black coal dust, the man turned and spit.

"I'm Darby Connors." He held his hand out and the old timer shook it. "I'm working on No. 46, the new shaft up top."

"I heard about that. Some proud work up there."

"Yeah, we're reinforcing everything real good," said Darby.

"Not like all these others," said the miner. "These others were built too fast and weren't made to last. They just want us in and out with the coal before the mountain shifts. Damn room and pillar mining. You cut it out and then pull the pillars and wonder why the roof caves in. Stupid."

"That's pretty dangerous," said Darby slowly.

"That's why we have one of these about every three or four months." He pointed at all the men still working frantically to clear the mine in the near distance.

"This happens a lot, then?" asked Darby.

"You can bet your last greenback. This happens all the time." He paused. "I've buried a lot of friends up here on this Godforsaken mountain mining coal. Twice a boy, once a man. You start out breaking coal as a boy, then you mine it as a man, and if you're one of the lucky ones to survive, you end up on top breakin' coal with the boys again." He paused briefly. "They say the country runs on coal. Well they need to slow it down before we're all killed."

Darby nodded his head to agree.

"You think we'll get these men out?"

"Yeah, we'll get 'em out. The question is whether or not they'll be breathin' when we do."

Darby looked out over the commotion. He had seen railroad accidents, but nothing like this. At least with a railroad accident you had daylight. Here, there was nothing but darkness, and inside the mine, there was pitch black and no oxygen.

Darby fell asleep from exhaustion. He was startled when they awakened him for another go. He worked his next shift and then fell asleep again. So much for no longer sleeping in work camps like at the railroad.

Food was brought in and served off long tables. Men who were dirty got more and more dirty. Tons of debris was extracted by hand, hour after hour. The sun came and went.

Then there was the yell.

"We're through!"

What was frantic before became more so.

One of the smallest men was sent in through a crawl space with a fuel lamp.

He was gone for an eternity as Darby knelt with his men briefly. They didn't want to disturb anything while the man was crawling into the cavity beyond. Then there were some voices. More than one--so somebody was alive.

Six men died in that accident. Twenty-nine survived. John Julias came out alive and Darby shook his hand as he crawled past and out toward fresh air. The six who perished were handed out and passed from man to man.

Darby did not know any of them but his heart sank to see them. Their wives, their girlfriends, their lovers would soon know and it would crush them.

Darby felt tears well up in his eyes, but he fought them back. Others were not so lucky, their faces streaked clean below their eyes.

The days and weeks that followed were different. There was a flurry of activity and some kind of government investigation. It didn't amount to anything. The official ruling was that it was a simple mining accident.

But that's not what most of the men thought, and when John Julias was made a scapegoat and fired, most were furious.

Julias was a good inside boss and the only reason he had gone into No. 32 was to inspect some of the support structure brought to his attention by the fire boss. The fire boss always entered the mine two hours before the men to check for gas and to look at what water might have done to weaken the ceiling and the walls. He had signed off on the mine but wanted Julias to go down and have a look at it while the men worked. It was known that Julias had learned some things from Darby-- the railroad man--and was more thorough in his inspections. Ironic that the ceiling collapsed when Julias was inside looking. Firing Julias was just

wrong. Hillten needed to blame somebody, so he blamed Julias.

Darby was promoted to inside
boss in the place of Julias. Some of the
men were happy to see that, while others were convinced he had no experience in the mines and would contribute
to killing them. A few quit, but not
many. Jobs were hard to get.

Darby met the owner of the company, a one Clarence Hillten, who he remembered as the man who was
receiving job applications on the day he
had applied and Mary was off helping
him. Maybe Hillten was Mary's father.
He was certainly grumpy--not nice at
all.

"I want the production to continue, Connors," said Hillten. "Get in
there and shore the gangways up but
don't slow down the production. We
have orders to fill."

"Yes sir, but I've seen some of
these gangways that are in pretty bad
shape. To do it right is going to take
some time," said Darby.

"I'm a businessman, Connors.

You know what a businessman does when production slows down?"

"No sir."

"He goes out of business, Connors. Do you know what that means, Connors? Do you know what happens when I go out of business?"

"No sir."

"You lose your job, Connors. You and all these other men. You all lose your jobs."

"Yes sir."

"So I want to run a safe mine but a quick mine. Do you understand me?"

"Yes sir."

"You get these gangways shored up but don't you interfere with my production."

"Yes sir, but when I move some big timbers in I have to use the tracks and you can't run the coal out when I'm moving timber in."

"I suggest you move fast, Connors. You haul out a load of coal and when they're digging more, you move your timbers in. Fast. Do you understand?"

"Yes sir, I'll do the best I can as fast as I can."

"Without production, Connors, there are no jobs. Tell the men that. You want to keep this mine open, you mine faster. All these repairs and delays cost us money. You understand that." The last line was not a question but a demand.

Darby did not like Hillten very much. He had seen owners like that on the railroad. They were all pretty much the same. Push, push, push, regardless of how many men got hurt.

When Darby left Hillten's office what seemed like the start of a bad day improved dramatically.

"Hello there," said Darby to Mary.

"Hello, Mr. Connors."

"You know my name?" replied Darby with some surprise.

"Filled out your job application, remember?" said Mary.

"I remember it like it was yesterday, Mary. Let's see, Mary of the Pittsburgh Mining Company, Limited."

"Oh, so you remember my name as well," she replied.

"I remember what you told me," he grinned.

"And that's more than most of these men ever know," she said with a little teasing tilt to her head.

Darby smiled.

"Well, as you may recall, I'm not like most of these men. I build railroad bridges and now I'm doing it for Mr. Hillten inside these mountains." Darby gestured toward the outside.

Mary's face turned a little tense when she heard the reference to Hillten.

"You mean *The Boss*," she mimicked, tossing her head to the side and rolling her eyes, "*The Boss* Mr. Clarence Hillten."

"Yes, Hillten," said Darby with a smile.

"Well I work with *The Boss* every day Mr. Connors, and I want to tell you..."

At that, Hillten's door swung

open and Hillten stood there glaring. He saw Darby flirting with Mary, if only for an instant.

"Mary, my office. And Connors, I thought I gave you a job to do."

"Yes, sir," said Darby as he turned and hurried out the door. He did not like that man.

The work proceeded well. Darby thrived under pressure. He knew what needed to be done and he encouraged his men to not only mine the coal, but also improve the safety. They liked that about him. Miners got paid by the load they sent up. Each car numbered in white chalk and the ticket boss above keeping track, pay was tied to the quality of the coal and the production. But safety was a concern for all the men below, and Darby was able to improve the gangways and at the same time keep the mules driving out the coal.

One man was killed in a dumb accident. He was a breaker boy, just 12 years old. Men were not supposed to ride on the spreader chain at the front of a cart being pulled out of the slope mine with the cable hoist. But he was, and when his soft miner's cap and fuel lamp flipped off his head he tried to reach down and grab it. He slipped and the car ran over him. The men at the engine house had no idea from the top cap what was happening down below where they couldn't see.

It wasn't Darby's slope and it wasn't his responsibility. He was inside boss for a shaft. But that didn't matter. The anguish of knowing that such a young life was taken away in an instant wrenched his gut.

On the train home, he cried for the boy. Why, he wondered, were such young boys being allowed to work in such dangerous places?

It was the work. People needed the work. The boy was probably helping to feed the family.

A hand touched Darby's shoulder.

"Mr. Connors?"

It was Mary.

Darby quickly rubbed the tears

out of his eyes.

"I cried, too," she said, fully understanding.

"I, ah," said Darby.

There was a silence.

"His name was Tim McLaughlin."

Darby looked at Mary standing beside him as the train swayed. He didn't know what to say. He felt his throat tighten.

"Did you know him?"

"No," said Darby.

"Did you even know his name?"

"No, I didn't," breathed Darby, trying to conceal another tear he felt welling up in his eye.

Mary patted his shoulder gently.

"It's all right."

Darby looked up at her and his eyes locked on hers. Tears rolled out of his eyes. Years of holding back things that happened flooded forward. He was embarrassed but there was no way he could stop it. He lowered his head and tears dropped onto his dirty overalls.

"May I sit down?" asked Mary.

Darby nodded his head and pointed to the smooth wooden seat across from him.

They sat in silence momentarily as Darby let the tears drop. Finally, he sniffled and wiped each eye one at a time. Mary just sat watching him. A tear slid from her eye.

"This coal mine is just so dangerous," said Darby eventually, with a bit of anger in his voice.

Mary nodded her head.

"What is a 12 year old boy doing riding the spreader chain?"

Mary didn't answer right away. She understood.

"What's a 12 year old boy doing in the mine in the first place?" she asked assertively. "The mine is no place for a boy."

"Half the breaker boys and the mule drivers are not much older," said Darby.

"They shouldn't be there at all," said Mary.

Darby looked directly into Mary's eyes. She looked back. Her blue eyes were older than her years. She knew. She understood.

"You work for Hillten. Can't you convince him that there are plenty of jobs for the boys up top?"

Mary tilted her head toward the floor. "He doesn't listen."

Darby didn't hear her well because of the clack-clack of the train. "What?"

"I said he doesn't listen. He won't listen. Mr. Hillten *The Boss* is a horse's ass."

Darby was surprised to hear her say that. He smiled.

"You don't like him very much," said Darby.

"How about if I say I don't like him at all?" responded Mary with assertion.

"That would be putting it plainly."

"Mr. Clarence Hillten is a horse's ass and a mean old slave driver who cares more about money than he does about you or Timothy McLaughlin, or me."

Darby smiled.

"That's putting it the way it is."

"As a matter of fact, that mouse of a man needs to be on this train right now instead of me," said Mary louder.

"Why?"

Mary held up an envelope that Darby had not noticed.

"I get to go tell Mr. and Mrs. McLaughlin why their boy isn't coming home this week. Now you would think that would be the job of the owner, wouldn't you? You'd think that would be the least he could do when one of the men he employs is killed in his stinking mine!"

Darby looked around the passenger car. There were only a few people riding, but one or two had heard her raised voice.

He didn't say anything but Mary could tell that he thought she was talking too loudly.

"They all know," she said looking around at the other passengers. "They all know what an evil man he is. They know Satan runs that mine."

Darby was shocked. Those were powerful words. He reached over toward Mary to calm her. She sighed loudly.

"I'm sorry, Mr. Connors. You are such a gentle man. You don't know what it is like being around someone who is as evil as he is."

Darby touched Mary's hand. At first it was a light grip and then he gave it a reassuring squeeze. Mary looked suddenly at Darby.

In his mind, Darby thought she would reprimand him, being so forward. He didn't consider his actions but rather just wanted to comfort her.

Mary approved. She didn't say anything, but her eyes thanked him. He held her hand a while longer. The train pulled into the station and he released his grip. Mary touched his hand as he pulled away. She stood up without speaking and turned to disembark.

Darby sat and watched as she and other passengers made their way for the door. Darby felt strange. Not since his beloved May had he had any

feelings like he was sensing at that moment. And yet, Mary was such a young
girl compared to him. His feelings had
to be wrong.

Mary glanced over at Darby
when she stepped out of the train.
Darby was busy getting his lunch pail
from under the bench and did not see
her.

But as she walked by outside the
rail car she looked in through the window. There, she caught Darby's eyes
watching for her. She hesitated and
then mouthed the words, "Thank you."

Darby was surprised to hear a
tap on his door at the boarding house a
few hours later. Hardly anyone ever
knocked on his door, especially after
dark. Imagine his surprise when he
opened his door to see Mary standing
there.

Her eyes spoke volumes. She
was hopeful.

Darby read her face.
"Mary! Come in!"
Mary hesitated, then stepped

through the door.

"What's wrong? How did you find me?"

Mary came in and helped herself to a chair setting next to the lone table in the room.

Darby looked around at his place apologetically. It was a man's apartment, and was far from neat.

"I read the address off your job application," said Mary.

"Oh," said Darby, wondering the purpose of the surprise visit.

"Would you like some water?" Darby asked.

"Sure," said Mary.

Darby poured water from a small can into a tin cup. He handed it to her. Mary took it with both hands and sipped.

"I guess you talked to Timothy McLaughlin's mother and father?"

Mary nodded her head.

"I bet that was rough," said Darby.

"There are no words to describe it."

Darby moved a trunk closer to the table and sat next to Mary.

"I don't see why you have to do that."

Mary openly cried.

"He had two little brothers," she said, starting to sob. "They had little faces and big brown eyes. Mr. McLaughlin sent them out of the room. Mrs. McLaughlin started screaming."

Darby reached out toward Mary and she responded by grabbing him and pulling him toward her. She buried her head in his shoulder and shook as she cried.

Darby patted her head. He had no idea what to say to her. He just held her.

Minutes passed before she calmed.

"He's such a bastard," she said. "I hate him."

Darby didn't answer immediately, but then, "Who?" he asked.

"My husband."

Darby released his grip a little.

"Your husband? I didn't..."

"Mr. Clarence Hillten, *Big Boss, Big Mine Owner.*" Mary paused. "My name is Mary Hillten," said the young girl.

Mary clutched Darby harder.

"I didn't know that," said Darby slowly.

"Nobody knows," she said. "He doesn't think people should know. He's evil."

"Hillten is your husband?"

"And my boss," said Mary with disgust.

"I just, I..." Darby was uncomfortable and tried to let go of Mary.

"Hold me," said Mary. "At least you're a man."

Darby gripped her.

After a quiet moment, Mary leaned back and looked at Darby.

"I've watched you when you've come in to talk to him. I know how he treats you, how he treats everybody. But you stand up to him and you stick up for the men and for the boys and for people like Timothy McLaughlin. You're a bigger man than he will ever be. He may be the owner, but he is nothing."

"I'm not sure if you should be here," said Darby.

"Don't get angry with me," said Mary.

"I'm not angry," returned Darby. "I didn't know you were married."

"It's all right, I'm not."

"I thought you just said Hillten was your husband."

"Oh he is. But we're not really married. He treats me like just another one of his employees. He's so hateful to me."

"But you are married to him."

"Yes, I'm married to him," said Mary, irritated. "Yes I am married to that miserable worm but I don't love him and he doesn't love me. He's never really loved me. I was just his young trophy and I was just stupid. He swooped me off my feet and I thought we'd have a wonderful life together. I was so young and I was really wrong about that!"

"I'm sorry," said Darby, his mind

reeling. This girl he admired was married and he didn't even know it.

Darby watched as she clutched him and leaned her head on his shoulder. He could feel her breathing and he felt nervous.

"Are you sure you should be here?" he asked finally.

"I want to be here."

Darby could not think. Mary was the first woman he had held in his arms since May and it felt awkward. He knew he had been attracted to her since the day he met her, but the news of her marriage to the mine's owner was unsettling. His insides flipped.

"That bastard sends me on these errands of horror and he does not care one bit about my feelings or what happens to me while I'm gone," said Mary with resignation in her voice.

Darby did not know what to do.

"Would you like some more water?" he asked.

"Thank you," said Mary as she leaned back.

Darby poured from his can into

her cup.

"You're such a kind man," said Mary.

Mary drank and then gripped Darby. He held her and rocked her. To her it was heaven. Darby was a man who cared. He was a man who put his arms around her when she was hurting and did not need to talk. His warmth made her feel safe.

They sat together for an hour or so and then Mary announced that she had to go. Darby watched her as she left and closed the door. He didn't quite know what to think, but he knew he felt a closeness with her. Yet he struggled terribly with the idea that she was married, and to, of all people, the boss.

The men at the mine were angry the next few days. At first no one knew Timothy McLaughlin's name, but it wasn't long before the name had become a cry for reform.

Darby was fairly new to mining, but he was not new to the pitiful conditions of labor. At the railroad, men were expendable. If the job got done, fine. If it didn't, labor was blamed. Regardless of the conditions, the work went on.

At the mine, it was the same, only worse. More men perished in coal mining in Pennsylvania than from any other cause. Hundreds of thousands worked around the country digging coal, feeding the post Civil War industrial giant. Immigrants continued to arrive in New York by the tens of thousands, and they were ready to work any job just to get a grip on the American Dream.

Talk started at the mine about organizing and the men turned to Darby for leadership. They wanted safety--more timber in the gangways, some kind of control over who does what in the mine, better handling of open flames, a first aid station inside for the inevitable accidents, and shorter hours. God knew they needed shorter hours. Darby listened carefully and agreed.

They could have all been fired for

such talk, but that did not stop them. Conditions had reached such a point that something had to be done.

Darby agreed to take the complaints to Mr. Hillten. Three of the other men agreed to go with him but only two showed up on the morning they planned to speak with the owner.

Milten Johnson was a miner and Mason Applebee worked the hoist house. Johnson was a burly man, typical of a coal digger, with a stout build, rough bearded face and cold eyes. Applebee was smaller, but still, a man used to working and toughened by the responsibility of hoisting men and mules up and down in the cage and bringing coal up by the cart load. It was a heavy responsibility lowering men hundreds of feet into the earth in a cage on a single cable. And it was dangerous. Things could go wrong.

As the three marched up the wooden steps that lead to the office, Darby rehearsed what he was planning to say. They were coming without an appointment, but they were confident Hillten would be in the office. It was payroll day and he was always in the office when the money was handed out. It was as if he had to touch every greenback and see to it that the absolute minimum was paid out to the men who did the dirty work for him.

Darby opened the door and stepped inside with Johnson and Applebee at his heels.

Mary sat at her desk and looked up when the three men arrived. Mary's eyes caught Darby's immediately and, without saying anything, she communicated, "What's going on?"

"May we speak to Mr. Hillten?" Darby asked without any hint that he was fond of Mary.

"Yes, sir," she replied. "Is there a problem in the mine?"

Darby did not want to answer.

"We need to take some matters up with Mr. Hillten." Darby tried to give Mary a reassuring smile. She was puzzled. She stood up and went into Hillten's office. The men heard him yell at her but they could not make out what Hillten said.

Mary emerged shaking.

"He doesn't want to see you. Payroll. He said take it up with the inside boss for your seam."

Darby stepped toward the door.

"Mr. Hillten, I *am* the inside boss," said Darby tentatively. He was not afraid of speaking up, but Mr. Hillten was a powerful man and it was dangerous to contradict him.

"Who the hell are you?" came a loud voice from inside the office.

"Darby Connors, inside boss for shaft 46."

"Somebody's been killed?" asked Hillten.

"No, sir," answered Darby. Then, he added, after a brief silence, "Not yet, sir."

The three men heard Hillten's heavy wooden chair move back away from the desk.

Mary quickly jumped into her seat at her desk. Johnson and Applebee stepped back. But Darby, Irish-railroad-man Darby, stood his place.

Hillten was angry for being interrupted. Actually, he was always angry, but on payroll day this was an inconvenience he did not like.

"What do you want?" he barked.

Darby stood tall.

"May we come in, sir?"

Hillten looked at Johnson, top to bottom. He knew Applebee, but he did not recognize Johnson.

"Who's this?" he said pointedly.

"That's Mr. Johnson, miner in 46."

"And I'm Mason Applebee, hoist engineer." Applebee extended his hand toward Hillten. Hillten did not shake it.

"I know who you are." Hillten looked over the men. "What do you want?"

"Could we come in to your office and discuss some safety matters?" asked Darby.

"There's nothing wrong with the safety in my mine," said Hillten succinctly.

"Sir, if we could just..." Darby began.

Hillten noticed Mary watching and grinning.

"What the hell are you looking at?" he snapped toward her.

Mary turned her head to look at the desk and started shuffling papers.

"In here," said Hillten as he retreated to his office. The men followed.

It was not a big office, but it was cluttered with crates and papers. There was a stack of money on the desk where Hillten had been counting it out.

He reached for the money and placed it in the desk drawer.

"You know I'm doing payroll. So make it quick."

Darby cleared his throat.

"Sir, the men have been discussing safety..."

"The men?" scoffed Hillten as he cut off Darby.

"Sir, the safety conditions..."

"What men are you talking about?"

"Sir, just about all the men."

"Is this union talk, Connors? You know I'll fire the three of you if this is union talk."

"Sir," continued Darby bravely, "this is about safety. We have safety problems all over the mine."

"I run a safe mine, everybody knows that," spouted Hillten, pointedly.

"With all due respect, sir, there are some things that need to be improved."

"Connors, do you know anything about running a business? I have payroll to meet. I can't do that when production slows down or when lazy men refuse to work."

"My men are not lazy," said Johnson.

"I'm not talking to you. I'm talking to Connors here," said Hillten.

Darby put his hand on Johnson's forearm to hold him back.

Johnson had obviously won plenty of bar fights in his day and it was clear he wanted to take Hillten down.

Applebee's knees started knocking and his face grew pale.

"Sir," said Darby, "the men don't believe young boys should be working deep in the mine. Put them atop to drive the mules there. Keep them in the breaker house."

"I don't need a railroad man to tell me how to run a mine!" shouted Hillten. "Is that what you're here to do? I should have known better than hire a railroad man. This country is going to hell!"

"No, sir, we are trying to increase production."

Hillten snapped his head toward the door where he could see Mary standing.

"What do you want?"

"I have the production figures here. Every time there is an accident, we produce less coal," said Mary.

"Get out of my office!" yelled Hillten. "All of you!"

Applebee shot out of the door like a bullet. Johnson stood shoulder to shoulder with Darby.

"This mine is dangerous as hell!" said Darby. "He's right!" said Johnson.

Hillten looked at them with his cold eyes.

Then, in a low voice he spoke.

"So you two are some kind of leaders. At least the hoist man had the sense to get out of here. Let me tell you something. There's a depression on. There are plenty of men to fill your shoes. I don't need some railroad has-been to tell me what's what in my mine. The driver boys work the mules on the gangways in the mine. They do that because they aren't strong enough to mine coal. When they get older they move up to dig dirt. Later, if the are good enough and if they work hard enough, some of them might become miners.

"As for you, railroad man, the only reason you're here is because you know how to handle timber. But I don't like your attitude. I don't like you organizing in my camp. Maybe you're with the Brotherhood of the Footboard. Maybe you're part of the National Labor Union. I don't know who you represent, but you will not represent the men that I hire! Do you understand me?"

Darby looked at him eye-to-eye.

"If I had a son I would never let him work in this hellhole!"

"If you had a son?" Hillten laughed. "Word is you don't have a son. Don't now and never will!"

"Well no son of mine would ever work for you!" said Darby loudly.

"So that's a threat, railroad man?"

"No sir, Mr. Hillten, that is a promise." Darby stared at Hillten and Hillten stared back.

"Get back to the shaft. Get some coal out of the ground. Consider your pay docked for the time you wasted in here."

Then he focused on Johnson. "As for you, miner, you're fired!"

Johnson lunged at Hillten but Darby caught him and wrestled him back.

"Get out of my office or I'll fire both of you! Get out!"

Darby pulled Johnson through the office door. Mary jumped up and opened the outside door. As Darby passed she stuffed some papers in Darby's hand.

Johnson was not happy about being fired and Applebee was nowhere to be seen. Darby clunked down the steps and then looked at the papers. They were production figures with dates and a list of accidents. He looked back toward the office and saw Mary trying to hurry him away. Darby could hear Hillten's rant from outside. Mary turned slowly and went back inside.

There was union talk after that, for certain. Within a week there was another accident; two men were injured and one killed. Darby did organize the men and someone from the National Labor Union was seen on the property. Hillten hired a security man, who fired shots at the man from the union.

The workers staged a slowdown. Less coal came out of the mine, but it only hurt the miners, who were paid according to the quality and production of their coal. Hillten fired anyone he caught talking union and made it clear that any drop in production would make it worse on everyone. They were already working a 12 hour day and Hillten threatened to increase it to 14 if production didn't pick up.

Darby made trips to see Hillten every day, always attempting to reason with the owner but seldom making any progress. He would speak to Mary as he came and went and sometimes she would hand him documents. A time or two their hands touched and lingered when the papers were handed off.

Every day on his way home on the train, Darby wondered and worried, about Mary. He could not imagine the hell she was living. How she ended up with such a monster for a husband was impossible to imagine. The production figures and other documents she gave Darby were conclusive proof that accidents slowed output and Darby used that to build his case for improved safety.

The men were indeed organizing for better conditions, and Darby became a threat to the ownership. He had a powerful voice and though he received no concessions from Hillten, his word with the men controlled production.

Then, one night, Mary soundly knocked on Darby's boarding house door. Darby opened it slowly, and then more quickly when he saw who it was.

"Mr. Connors," said Mary with dread in her voice.

"Come in," said Darby.

"Mr. Connors, you must watch yourself."

Darby looked both ways down the hallway near his room. He closed the door.

"What's wrong?"

"There are men looking for you," said Mary. "Men he's hired to stop you."

"Mr. Hillten hired somebody?"

"Yes! That bastard," she said. Without warning, Mary lunged toward Darby and hugged him tightly.

Darby held her.

"How do you know this?"

Mary started to cry. Darby held her and she placed her head on his chest.

Finally, Mary released her grip slightly and looked up at Darby. Her eyes concentrated on Darby's eyes.

"I'm in love with you," she said softly.

Darby's heart thumped in his chest. How could this woman know how he felt?

"I get a feeling in my stomach when I think about you," she said.

Darby clutched her tightly.

"I think about you all the time," said Darby softly. "Sometimes I think about you too much."

Mary felt flush. Darby's embrace was so strong and loving--something she desperately needed. She didn't want to let this man go. Mary leaned back to look at Darby's face.

"I respect you, Mr. Connors. And I'm so attracted to you. You're everything I want in a man. And right now I want to kiss you."

Darby looked at her as she

slowly leaned toward him and kissed him.

"A little kiss," she said.

Darby reached over and put his hand under her chin and they kissed a second time, tongues touching. Mary bit down on Darby's lip.

Mary's breathing was quickened and Darby saw her heartbeat in the blood vessels of her neck.

Mary gripped Darby as she put her head on his chest. He stroked her hair.

"I had to come to you and tell you."

"I love you, too," he whispered. "I've loved you since those first days."

Mary kissed Darby again.

"I've wanted this," said Darby.

"Take me away from here," she said.

"I think about you and I worry about you."

"I want to be with you, Darby."

Darby smiled to himself as Mary tried to nestle herself in his arms. He didn't think he had ever heard her call him by his first name.

Then, she looked up at him with a glow in her eyes.

"I want to make a baby with you. I want to give you a son. He'll never have to work in this mine and that bastard can go to hell."

Darby felt a powerful emotion come over him. He never had a son, and he wanted one, but after May died he didn't want to be with any other woman. Mary, though--Mary was different than all the rest. Mary was special. Mary was tough and beautiful and she was lonely and afraid and she wanted to be the mother of his child--a gift that he never thought anyone would give him. It was a generous gift, a loving gift, a gift that only she could grant him.

"I, I don't know what to say," said Darby. "I don't know what to say to you Mary of the Pittsburgh Mining Company, Limited."

"I think about you and I feel, I feel you physically," she said. "I've thought about coming to you so many times."

"But you're married and it's so..." said Darby.

"I don't care. You don't have a son, but you deserve one more than any man I know. I'm in love with you and I want your baby. No one has to know."

The two loved each other that night and all their worries disappeared. The magic, the passion, the love, the trust--all the emotions were there. They were one.

Darby removed a leather note-book from the counter and opened to a blank page. With an old pencil he traced around his hand and then placed Mary's hand over the image from his and traced around hers.

"You are the sweetest and most loving girl I have ever known," Darby whispered quietly to Mary. "The tender moments we shared tonight will never leave my mind. We will always know each other and I will love you for the rest of eternity."

Darby Connors was killed in a

mining "accident" the next day. As he was being lowered into shaft No. 46, the cable somehow came disengaged and the cage fell 400 feet to the bottom of the seam. There was an investigation, but nobody was charged with murder, though foul play was suspected. Half the miners walked off the job and soon the mine was closed for lack of labor.

Mary left the Pittsburgh Mining Company, Limited, before nightfall the day Darby was killed, in shock, and she was never seen in Pennsylvania again. She had a son, who grew up never having breathed coal dust, or ever having heard the cruel voice of Clarence Hillten. Sadly, the boy also never knew his real father.

As for Clarence Hillten, after the mine closed and Mary left, he drank himself to death, slowly, as a lonely man should and as he deserved.

Mary found and took the leather notebook from Darby's apartment on her way out of town and in it she read some words she thought about for years: "LOOK FOR ME. I WILL FIND YOU." She didn't know what they meant or who wrote them, but she yearned for Darby the rest of her days.

Chapter 8

April 5, 1956
Hollywood, California

"Unbelievable! She is just plain impossible! I will not, under any circumstances, work with her. No way!"

The door slammed so hard that the glass shattered and fell to the ground. David Ross looked at the glass around his feet.

"I'd say that was a splendid experience," he muttered to himself.

David brushed the hair out of his eyes and stood, momentarily, considering his next move. Medium frame, thin and handsome, his hands held up a couple of pages which represented his latest proposal.

The voice inside the room noticed that David was still standing outside the office.

"Get the hell out of here!"

"Thank you," said David sarcastically. "I don't suppose..."

"Get ouuuuuut!!"

"Didn't think so."

David put his hand in the pocket of his slacks, fumbling for his car keys. He was dressed to meet the big studio executive about a photo project he had hoped to do but it appeared he was now pretty much over-dressed. His brown hair constantly fell onto his forehead and his boyish looks understated his wisdom.

As a young photographer, he had had a little success here and there, but his big goal was to do a photo shoot with the great film star Misty Adams.

Misty Adams was a legend. She came up as a young actress doing B films in the 1940s but was so loved by the public that nothing could keep her off the big screen, except, maybe herself.

Maybe Misty Adams had gotten too big. Once she became an A list actress, there were all kinds of rumors about how crazy she was, how "hard she was to work with," as they say. Some of the directors wouldn't even consider working with her despite the fact that she had fans everywhere. She'd show up late or not at all and any picture she was on came in over budget.

Some of the talk around town was that she was such a problem that she would not work again. She wasn't worth the risk. She was yesterday's news.

David didn't think so. He didn't even know her, but his idea was that she should return to her roots. Do a big modeling spread for one of the national magazines and a tell-all article. Explain to people that the reason she was so good on screen is because she put everything into her craft--everything. She was difficult off screen because she worked so hard to make her performances perfect. Plus, David's idea was to make a film documentary of the photo shoot--something that could be run in the theaters and promote her as a person--the woman behind the star.

Of course, David wasn't doing too well selling the idea. Misty Adams' reputation was so bad that the studio executives didn't even want to entertain the concept of trying to bring her back.

But then, what did David know? He wasn't her agent. He wasn't anything to her. He had never even met her. He was just a photographer from New York with a lofty idea. There were plenty of those around.

David had a little apartment not far from Paramount, and it was not uncommon for him to glimpse one or more of the Hollywood greats on their way to and from work. He saw Frank Sinatra, Bob Hope, Gary Cooper, even a young Jerry Lewis.

But when it came to Misty Adams, David had never seen her and he determined that if he was going to do a photo shoot of her he had better figure out a way to meet her. Approaching the studios wasn't working. All of them had had enough of her and while she was not actually black-listed, mention of her name invoked highly emotional reactions.

David stepped into a diner near where he lived and ordered eggs and corn. It was an odd combination for lunch but he liked it and the gal across the counter had long since given up trying to persuade him against it.

"Here you go, David," said Linda Billings. She was brunette, a little short gal with light skin, but pleasant enough. She slid a plate over to David's spot.

"Thank you, Linda," he replied.

Linda wiped the counter with an old rag that should have been thrown out, or at least laundered, about a month before.

"What 'ja workin' on these days?" Linda sort of liked David. He was a regular, and single, and he had what she considered to be an exciting job, photographer to the stars.

"Oh, I'm still trying to arrange a

photo shoot of Misty Adams."

"She is so beautiful," said Linda. "What I wouldn't do to be in her shoes."

"I understand it is not as fun as it looks," said David.

"Oh, yeah, I'm sure getting your picture taken all day long and having men roll out the red carpet for your limo gets real boring."

David looked up and smiled at Linda. He knew she was being sarcastic in her own way.

"No, really. She's under a lot of pressure. An actress like Misty Adams has all kinds of meetings to make and she has to memorize scripts and there are people all around her. You know she never gets a day off."

"I think I could handle that," said Linda. "Everybody wanting your picture, asking for your autograph--you being the most important thing in the room."

David looked up from his plate to reach for ketchup.

"What about you, you're doing a little acting aren't you?"

"Huh. The only acting I do is when my boyfriend puts his hands all over me. I show him a good time."

"Oh?" asked David. "I thought you were taking acting classes."

"No," said Linda. "But I am going to sign up for some."

"See, so you're on your way."

Linda leaned over the counter to expose her cleavage just a little. The waitress outfit she was wearing was not all that attractive, especially with a few stains on the blouse.

"You'd take my picture, wouldn't you, David?" asked Linda in as seductive a voice as she could muster.

David looked up at her and gave her the once-over. "Maybe one of these days. But you better start on those acting classes as fast as you can."

Linda wiggled a little. "Maybe I'm not Misty Adams, but I'm here for you any time you want to get some sexy pictures."

David pushed the plate to the side. He had cleaned it.

"Linda, I will certainly keep that

in mind. But today, young lady, I am on a quest to photograph one of the biggest stars in Hollywood. Your day will come." David slid two dollars in coins toward her.

"Thank you, David."

"You keep that change and put it in your piggy bank for those acting lessons."

"I will certainly do that," she said. She pushed a nickel back. It was a 1928 Buffalo. "Keep this one for luck," she said. David smiled.

David gathered his things and left the diner. It was a beautiful Hollywood day, nice and warm, sun shining. David looked right. Then he looked left. It was a big town and somewhere out there was his prey.

According to *Variety* magazine, Misty Adams lived in Hollywood. Her mansion was off one of those winding roads through Hollywood Hills and David had pretty much figured out which gate led up to her house. He had driven by it dozens of times, but he never even got a glimpse of her car or anybody else out in the yard.

The house had a big hedge around it and the gate was made of tightly spaced steel spires. There was no way to break in, jumping the fence was out of the question.

David even pressed the doorbell at the gate a few times and tried to talk his way in as a flower delivery man, a courier bringing bad news from Western Union and one time he even rented a limo and tried to make out like he was a Paramount executive.

Evidently Misty Adams was hip to all the tricks because not once did the gate open to admit him.

So it was a beautiful day in Hollywood and David didn't have a clue how he was going to meet the biggest, or, once biggest star, in Tinseltown.

He stepped slowly over to his Packard, black, of course, left over from World War II and not exactly the kind of flashy car that it takes to be noticed in Hollywood.

David opened the door with a

creak and climbed into the driver's seat.

He thumped his fingers on the steering wheel, glanced at his camera gear in the back seat.

How could he do it? How could he set up a photo shoot with Misty Adams? It wouldn't be easy.

He started the engine and figured that he would cruise by her house and just see if an idea popped in his head. It was such a great day. Maybe she'd be out in the yard getting some sun.

David liked this part of the year. Because of the Pacific Ocean it was cool during the day but still very warm at night. He was kind of a night person anyway, and he liked it when the evenings were the right temperature. Oddly, though, a photographer deals in light and he liked the darkness. But then, maybe that is why he felt comfortable processing his pictures in the darkroom. He didn't mind it, even liked the smell of the chemicals, and darkroom work put him totally into the world that he had photographed when he was working with any particular set of pictures.

And yes, he had photographed some pretty girls in his day, every photographer in his line of work had. There were a lot of women in Hollywood who wanted to be Misty Adams and every one of them was ready to pose for pictures.

It seemed like being a photographer was a direct route to their heart. It took a lot to model and while David was working with his subjects it was quiet time together with them. If he could make them look good, they adored him.

Of course, that wasn't always possible. Some girls were just not born good-looking. It was a fact of nature. No photographer could make some girls look good. There were no tricks, no angles, no lighting conditions that would make a disproportionate face look appealing.

That's what David liked about Misty Adams. God built her right. God did his best work when he made that number.

David's daydreaming had occupied him just about all the way up to her house, and, as expected, he saw nothing. There was no one in the yard, no car in the drive, no sign of life at all.

How could Misty Adams spend all day, every day, sequestered in her house?

David slowly passed on by. What then?

He drove about a quarter mile past the house and pulled off the road where people tended to turn around. He let the motor run briefly and then turned it off.

Instinctively he opened the door to let a little of the engine heat float out of the passenger area. The big, wide seats felt a little warm to him, so David stepped out of the car and stood, looking up and down the street.

An idea, he needed an idea. He had thought about getting a job as a waiter at a restaurant that Misty Adams had been seen at before. He even thought about getting a job at the hotel where she stayed in Los Angeles from time to time.

But how long would that take? He couldn't wait around a year on the off chance that she would show up and he happen to be there and she happen to run into him and they happen to strike up a conversation. Pointless.

David was absolutely drawing a blank. He could attend a premier of one of her movies, except she wasn't making any movies at the moment. That was the problem. She had been overplayed and she had bitched out one too many directors. No premiers, no celebrity parties.

Hey, thought David, what about a charity? What charity did she support? Maybe he could go to work for them. But no, last he remembered she was big on feeding the poor in Africa. That's a pretty big place and where would he go hang out on a deal like that?

David got back into his car and cranked the engine.

He signaled and pulled out into the road.

Just then, there was a sudden honk, a long, blaring honk and a limousine swerved to miss him.

David jumped and in the process turned off the engine. The passenger side window was open on the limo and if David wasn't mistaken, he thought he caught a glimpse of somebody with long blonde hair.

He cranked the engine while the limo moved on down a curve. In his zeal, his foot then slipped off the clutch and the car jumped and stalled. The limo disappeared around a curve.

"Damn it!" said David aloud.

He fumbled to start the car and when he got it going, the engine roared.

If that was Misty Adams, this was a chance of a lifetime.

He negotiated the curves rather quickly but the limo had driven out of sight.

Lucky for David, there were no major turns off the road so all he had to do was catch up.

David concentrated and pushed the speed. A time or two he caught a glimpse of the limo as it made its way out of the hills.

David almost lost traction on one curve and slowed for the next. It would not do him any good if he wound up in the ravine. His heart pumped adrenaline through his blood stream.

This was it, he knew it. This was his chance. All he had to do was follow that car and wherever it was going, he was going, and he'd try to meet her when she got to her destination.

David's camera gear shifted in the back seat as he made another fast turn.

A few more curves and he'd be directly behind the limo. Faster, faster, yet safe.

"Be safe, be safe," David said to himself.

He knew, though, that they were getting closer and closer to the main highway and if he didn't catch up to her he would not see which way she turned.

David pressed on the accelerator.

The wind blew in the window and made his hair fly. A few more turns. Just a few more turns.

"Damn, damn, damn it!" said David as he came up to the highway. He looked both ways and could not see the limo. Did she go right toward downtown or left toward Griffith Park? Was it left or was it right? It was fifty-fifty.

"Damn it!" repeated David.

He sat at the intersection scanning both directions.

"It's a nice day, it's a nice day," he said almost as an epiphany. "It's a nice day and she's going to the park. She's going to the park."

David stepped on the accelerator and peeled out to the left. The park it would be. Surely she was headed to the park on such a beautiful day. He would meet her, he would propose the project, she'd say "yes" and that would be that. He'd have the job and both of their careers would move forward.

David drove to the park with all dispatch. When he arrived, there was a labyrinth of roads. Which way did she

go? Where did she go? What's her favorite spot? Where would a celebrity go
to visit the park and still have some pri-
vacy?

David tooled around slowly,
scanning all the side trails and picnic
tables. He looked up and down and he
looked back and he looked forward.

There was no sign of Misty
Adams. There was no limo and there
was no actress.

David finally pulled his car into
the shade under a big tree.

"Well that was a lot of fun," he
said. "That was great. She must have
gone downtown."

David sighed. He was right. It
was fun. It was the closest he had ever
been to her. But instead of keeping up
with her, he lost her. Instead of taking
a picture when she zoomed by, he fumbled starting his car.

Well, the day had shaped up
rather nicely, he thought.

David left the door open to his
car and he sauntered over to a picnic
table. There, he climbed on top and let

his body relax. It was indeed a nice day! He sneered at the thought. Maybe he just needed a nap.

David didn't look to see what time it was when he stretched out on the table so he did not know how long he had been there when he woke up. It was getting close to sunset so he was surprised to see how dark it had gotten. It wasn't completely dark, but it was darker than he had expected.

He popped up and looked at his car. The door was still standing open.

"Gosh," he said to himself.

David walked over to the car as he stretched and yawned. Boy, what a nap. Now the issue was food. Nothing in Griffith Park to be found.

David got in the car and closed the door with a heavy clatter. Packards were certainly a massive piece of steel.

David drove out of the park and then grabbed the road through Beverly Hills and to Santa Monica. It was a straight shot. A pretty night, David thought, and he'd get something to eat near the beach. Maybe he'd even take the camera out and shoot a couple of pictures of the moon as it came up over the city.

As the sun set over the ocean, David was reminded why he lived in California. Beautiful, beautiful sunsets every day, he thought. And it was a most spectacular sunset this night.

David bought a burger at a little hop near the ocean. Some girl on roller skates shoved her boobs into his window and served him.

He smiled to himself. "You gotta love LA."

Before heading back home David thought he'd go park by the beach and take a walk. He could see the seagulls gliding in the ocean air.

David loved the smell of the air and the salty breeze that lapped his face. This was paradise.

He walked with his camera and tripod as the sun left just a sliver of orange on the horizon. A time or two he stopped to make a picture. He was shooting Kodachrome. The sky was beautiful and the stars were starting to make themselves visible.

What started out as a short walk ended up being a long one. David was drawn to the ocean and he enjoyed trudging through the sand.

Occasionally, he would pass a couple necking and a few people sitting around a campfire. Hellos would be exchanged.

Tiring, David was just about to turn around when he saw a figure splashing in the surf. She was there by herself and by then the stars were full and a half moon had climbed into the sky behind him.

David sat in the sand to rest and to watch.

Odd, this woman out there by herself, actually in the water after dark.

He watched intently to get a better look at her but it was just too dark. A young woman, he could tell that, but from the distance he couldn't discern much else, except, well, except, she looked naked.

"I do love this place," David

smiled to himself.

A minute or two later the woman came out of the water and gathered up what looked like her clothes. She put some shorts on and some kind of jacket. She walked up the beach as the waves lapped her from behind. In one hand she carried a wet shirt.

David watched as she walked directly toward him. She hadn't seen him. He put his camera behind his back. He hadn't used it, but he sure didn't want her to think he had.

She came closer, closer, until...

"Ah," she said with a startle. She laughed. "I didn't see you there."

"I'm sorry ma'am," said David. "I just sat down and didn't notice you until you walked up."

"You didn't notice me?" she giggled. "You must be the only man in America."

"What?" said David.

"Never mind. What are you doing out here all alone?" she said in a coy voice.

"I guess I should be asking you

that," said David.

"How about if I sit down and let's talk about our loneliness," she said.

"Fine by me."

The girl stepped even closer and held her wet clothes over David's head and dripped on him.

"You want to go swimming with me?" she asked.

David looked at the woman closely. Her hair was all wet, her make-up was gone, it was dark.

"Oh my God," he said.

"What, you can't swim?" she asked playfully.

"No, yes, I mean, yes, I can swim. Are you...?"

"Yes, I am," she said. "I'm pleased to meet you. Who are you?"

"David."

"And who do you think I am?" she asked as she dropped down in the sand beside David.

"Well, ah, well, you sure look a whole lot like Misty Adams, the big star."

"And you would be right, except

for the big star part. I am Misty Adams the former star and I've had a glass of wine this evening and I'm a little bit drunk."

"Amazing," said David.

"That's what they say about me. I am pretty amazing, except when I'm drunk and when I'm drunk I am more than amazing."

"Unbelievable," said David.

"That too," said Misty. "I am unbelievable when I am drunk. You're not with the press are you?" she asked.

David leaned back on his camera. "No, the paparazzi, no. Not at all."

"Well, I see the tripod," said Misty, "so I figure you are one of the press stalkers."

"No, not me. I mean, well, I am a photographer, but I'm not with the press or the paparazzi or any of those people. I just, I take pictures. I, I photographed that sunset this evening."

"Oh, wasn't it tremendous?" asked Misty as she fell back in the sand with her arms outstretched. "I love to swim at sunset."

"Well," said David, not really knowing what to say, "you certainly had a beautiful sunset this evening."

Misty lay silent for a moment.

"Isn't it beautiful?" she asked as she looked up at the stars in the sky.

"Yes, it is," said David looking up.

"Hey, do you want to take a swim?"

"Well, I, ah, yes, sure I'd love to swim."

"I'm skinny dipping you know," said Misty.

"That's okay by me."

"You don't have to take your clothes off," she said playfully. "But if you do, I won't tell anyone."

David smiled.

"Are you sure you are Misty Adams?" he asked.

"Oh, I'm sure," she replied. "I am the legend of the silver screen."

"Amazing."

"I think you already said that."

"Well I just, you know you just never..."

"Hey young fella, I'm a people too. What did you say your name was?"

"David."

"Well, David," said Misty, "if you want to go skinny dipping with Misty Adams, I suggest you start taking off your clothes."

Misty rolled to her side and then stood up. She pulled off her shorts, dropped her jacket and started off toward the beach.

David couldn't believe it. He wanted to take a picture to prove what he was seeing but he didn't dare. Instead, he slipped off his clothes and followed Misty toward the water.

By the time he arrived, she was already splashing in the surf.

Slowly, he moved toward the water. When it hit him, it felt warm. Then, the wind blew on his wet skin and he felt a little cool.

"Come on in," said Misty in the darkness.

David could see the sky glow reflect off the waves as they crashed in and the white caps shone white.

"Water feels great," David said.

"So I'm right!" said Misty.

"Yes. About what?"

"Skinny dipping is pretty fabulous."

"Yes it is," he said as David was hit by a wave a little bigger than he expected. He was pushed to his knees and then over. Momentarily his head went under water. Misty laughed at the sight.

"Well, you certainly are a good swimmer," she teased.

"Yeah," he said as he wiped water off of his face.

"What did you say your name was again?" asked Misty.

"David."

"That's right, David. Well, David," said Misty, "I bet you didn't think this morning when you woke up that you'd be naked in the ocean with Misty Adams."

"No, I sure didn't," said David, concealing his secret interest in meeting her.

"I bet you didn't even know I existed," said Misty.

"Oh yeah, sure I did. I've seen all your movies."

"Liar," she said with a grin.

"No, I have."

"You couldn't have seen all my movies. The studio hasn't released the last one."

"Oh? Why's that?"

"I guess it wasn't finished." Misty giggled.

"Why not?"

"I walked off the set."

David did know about that. It was in all the trade magazines.

"So why did you do that?"

"I got my period."

"What?" David wasn't sure of what he thought he heard.

"My period, you know, the curse. They wanted me to do a love scene when I was cramping so bad I couldn't even think. So I told director Horace Jacobs that he could finish the picture without me."

"Wow! I see."

A wave crashed over Misty's

shoulders.

"C'mon," she said, "I'm cold."

She stood up in the water and for the first time David got a good look at her breasts up close. It was dark, but he could certainly see everything. She turned and splashed toward the beach.

David stood up and bashfully walked behind her.

She found her clothes and wiggled into them as David came up behind.

"That was fun, wasn't it?" she asked.

"Yes." David fumbled to put his clothes on as Misty continued dressing.

"Well I guess I better go," she announced.

David didn't know what to do.

"Wait," he said almost desperately. "Don't run off."

Misty turned to look at him.

"You are pretty cute."

"Come on, sit with me," David said persuasively.

Misty stepped toward him.

"Well, if you put it that way. But

I must say, I sure would like a glass of wine."

"I don't have any wine."

"No wine? Then why should we stay here? Men who don't bring me wine don't keep me very long."

"Well, I wasn't planning..."

"Yes, I know," said Misty as she sat down beside David.

"You're the luckiest photographer in the world. Do you know how many photographers would kill to be in your shoes right now? But then, you're not wearing any shoes."

"I have them. They're here somewhere."

"No wine and no shoes. What can you do for a girl who loves wine and shoes, and you don't have either one?"

"We can talk," said David.

Misty laughed.

"You are different," she said. "I will give you that. Every other man in the world would have said something else."

"I..."

"You're nervous, that's what you

are."

"Yeah, well, I didn't plan this."

Misty moved a little closer to David. Even in the dim light he could see her incredible beauty.

"If you could do anything in the world," said Misty, "what would you do right now?"

David had no idea how to answer that question.

"I, ah, I guess I would just sit here and get to know you."

Misty moved her face closer to David's.

"That's a very good answer. You know I just hate men who are in love with me and don't know a thing about me. You're different."

"Well, I just--I guess I just respect you more than most."

"That's pretty rare."

David leaned back in the sand and turned to face Misty.

"So, Misty Adams, where were you born?"

Misty laughed.

"You are something!" she said.

"I just thought we should start at the beginning," he said.

"Very good. That's true." She paused to adjust herself in the sand to face David the way he was facing her.

"I was born right here."

David pretended to be surprised. "Here? On this beach?"

Misty tapped him on the shoulder with her left hand. "No, silly, in Los Angeles."

"Oh, well, I thought you meant here on the sand."

Misty rolled back to lay flat on her back. "That would be something. Can you imagine being born right here on this beach?"

"I guess it has probably happened before."

"I suppose it could happen. Babies just pop out when they get ready, don't they?"

"Yeah, they do."

Misty yawned.

"I'm so tired."

David repositioned himself so that he could lay flat and look up at the stars.

"Do you ever wonder about the stars?" David asked.

Misty did not answer. She started to doze.

David looked at her.

"I guess not," he said.

He rolled back to look at the stars again. *If it was easy, everyone would be doing it.* It was a strange thought that was stuck in his head.

"What a difference a day makes," he said.

"What did you say?" asked Misty.

"Nothing," said David. "I was just talking to myself. I do that a lot."

"Aohh," said Misty sympathetically.

There was a brief silence.

"I think we should just sleep here," said Misty.

"Okay by me," said David.

Misty didn't answer. She was tired and drunk and this man she didn't know seemed harmless enough. She drifted off to sleep.

David listened to the ocean for

awhile and he thought about his incredible luck. What were the chances? He had looked for Misty Adams for months and now he was on the beach beside her. He had been skinny dipping with her and he was on the sand next to her while she was sleeping.

David half expected Misty to wake up at any time, but she didn't. In time, too, David's eyelids grew heavy and he fell asleep.

Imagine David's surprise the next morning when he awakened to seagulls flying above and the noise of some fishermen casting off the beach.

David was startled and a little disoriented at first, but then he remembered, Misty Adams!

He turned, but she wasn't there. David sat up and looked around. No Misty. He scanned the water to see if she was taking a swim. Nothing.

Disappointment rushed in. "Where is she?" he said quietly.

As the realization hit that she had gone, David cursed.

"What the hell?" Nobody would believe this story. David didn't even believe it.

David reached up and rubbed his face. Amazing how slimy you feel after sleeping on the beach. The salt air deposits a goo on everything.

David's mouth was dry and he was far from rested. The sand was nice, but it was in everything and David felt grimy. He could take a swim, but no, it was cooler than the night before and he just resolved to get up and walk back to his car.

David scanned the beach for Misty as he walked but she wasn't anywhere.

"Imagine that," he said. He found her by happenstance and then he lost her by falling asleep. That doesn't happen every day. And, not one single picture. Some photographer he was.

David had a headache and he reached up to rub his forehead. Something was on his face that looked like blood when he looked on his hand. Maybe mosquitoes drilled him all night long.

What an idiot. He felt like an idiot. There was no proof and no chance of that ever happening again.

David made it back to his car, tired and frustrated.

He opened the door and placed his camera equipment on the seat.

"Breakfast," he said aloud.

David wondered what time it was. It was just getting light. He wondered if anything would be open.

The little diner he had eaten at the previous evening was closed so he drove on back to his place. He knew Linda would be open. God, she would freak if she knew where he spent the night! She wouldn't believe it, though, and David was not about to tell her.

David walked into the diner and took a seat on his favorite stool.

Linda noticed him right away.

"What happened to you?"

"You wouldn't believe it if I told you," said David.

"What's wrong with your face?"

"What do you mean?"

"What's on your face?"

David reached up and rubbed his face and then looked at his hand.

Linda grabbed his wrist and stopped him. Then she laughed.

"Ha, ha!" she said. "You got drunk!"

"No, I didn't."

"Well you have lipstick all over your face, ha, ha."

David grabbed a coffee pot and tried to see his reflection in it. He could see the red.

"What is this?"

"I'm guessing the phone number of some dish you spent the night with." Linda got a big kick out of it.

"What?" asked David.

"There's a number on your face," said Linda, "In lipstick, except..." She squinted.

"Except, you can't read all of it."

"What does it say?" asked David excitedly.

"Looks like a 4, and a 5557."

"What? That's all, no exchange?"

"Just numbers. Of course you've

messed up the last two numbers, could be a 6 and a 1."

Linda looked closer and touched David's face as she tried to make out the numbers more closely.

"Yep, definitely 4, 5, 5, and that's either a 6, 1 or a 5, 7." Linda wrote the numbers on her order pad and slid it toward David.

David looked at it. No telephone exchange. But that was no problem. He could call all the different exchanges.

Linda brushed his hair and sand fell on the counter.

"What'd you do, get drunk on the beach?"

"You wouldn't..."

"Believe me," Linda finished his sentence. She smiled. "You are a mess."

David looked at the number on the pad again.

"Are you having second thoughts?"

"What?"

"Was she good?" asked Linda.

"No, it's not like that."

"Oh, so you didn't like her. Too bad."

"No," protested David, "it's not like that at all. I just met her and we talked."

"Well, I don't know about that. You must have been pretty drunk for her to write her number on your face. But it looks to me like she liked you."

David smiled.

"I don't know."

"Huh-huh. David's in love."

"Stop."

"I know the look. You're completely trashed, you have lipstick all over you, and a very pretty shade, and you don't know what happened, but you act like you're in a daze."

David looked at Linda and smiled.

"Can a man get a cup of coffee in a joint like this?"

Linda turned. "David's in love. Coffee coming right up."

David drank his coffee in relative

silence and then left to go back home. He looked in the mirror and compared the numbers on his face with the ones Linda had written on the pad. He just wanted to make sure he had them right. The last two digits were pretty smudged and he would just have to guess at those.

He was glad for a shower. It is amazing how much sand you can bring home when you sleep on the beach.

All David could think about was getting in touch with Misty Adams. He had the number, most of it, and since she gave it to him, surely she wanted to hear from him.

He looked at the clock. It was 9:30. It was still early. Should he call right away? Or, should he wait? Misty Adams may have done the same thing he did, went home, took a bath, maybe gotten something to eat.

He'd call her at 10:00.

That thirty minutes crawled by. David rehearsed what he was going to say.

"I'm the guy from the beach last

night. No. She knows that. Hi, I'm David from the beach. No. Not that. Hello, Miss Adams, I'm calling about the number you wrote on my face."

David chuckled. Sometimes he even made himself laugh.

Precisely at 10:00 David resolved to place the call. But then, what was the exchange? There were a lot of exchanges in the city. But then wait, he knew exactly where she lived, he could figure out the exchange.

David opened his well-worn phone book. He scanned for a map. Hollywood Hills was clearly marked. The exchange was Taylor, like Elizabeth Taylor.

So the number had to be TA4-5557 or TA4-5561. How hard could that be? It was one or the other.

David called the first number. It rang. And it rang, finally, someone picked up.

"Hello?"

"Hi, this is David, could I speak with Miss Adams please?"

"Who?"

"Miss Adams, is this the residence of Miss Adams?"

"I don't know what you're talking about," said an elderly voice.

"I'm sorry," said David, "I must have dialed the wrong number."

David hung up and swallowed. Okay, only one number to go. He dialed. Then he heard the rings. The phone was answered momentarily.

"Joe's Garage," said a male voice.

"Ah, yes sir," said David. "I'd like to speak with Misty Adams please."

"Yeah, right, buster, who wouldn't?"

"I was given this number," said David.

David heard the man muffle the phone and then talk to the other men in his shop. "Any a youse got Misty Adams hidden out anywhere?" The men laughed.

David was about to hang up when the man unmuffled the phone.

"There's no Misty Adams here. Less Julio is holding out on us." There was more laughter.

"Thank you," said David as he hung up. He felt humiliated.

Two numbers, two strikes.

David studied the slip of paper. Maybe Linda read it wrong. But then, he confirmed. Everything was pretty clear except the last two digits.

The last digit was either a 1 or a 7. The second to the last digit was either a 5 or a 6. He called both numbers.

But then it hit David. There were a possible four combinations, a 1, 7; a 1, 6; a 5, 7; and a 5, 6. He had only tried two of the four possibilities.

David dialed. Two to go.

David listened intently as the phone rang. A woman picked up.

"Hi, honey."

"This is David."

"Hi there, David."

David could hear some moaning in the background and some bad music.

"Is this Misty?"

"Do you want me to be?" said a sexy voice.

"Not unless you are."

"Who do you want me to be?"

asked the girl.

"I want you to be who you are."

"I'm Puffin, but I can play Misty."

"Well, no," said David, "I'm looking for Misty. Is she there?"

"No, I don't think so."

David listened to the noise in the background.

"What are you doing?"

"We're making a movie, do you want to come?"

"No, I don't think so."

"We always need extras."

"No, I don't think so. Are you sure there isn't a Misty there?"

"No," said the chick, "It's just me and Dreamie."

"Dreamie?"

"Yes, don't you want to come see us?"

"What kind of a name is Dreamie?"

"I like it. She's really pretty. I just did a scene with her."

David smiled to himself.

"Well, not today. I'm trying to locate someone else. But I'll keep your number."

"All right then, Davy, I'll be waiting."

"Bye."

Puffin made a kissing sound on the phone as David hung up.

"This is a great country," said David to himself.

He dialed the next number nervously. This had to be it. This had to be Misty Adams' number. One ring. Two rings. Three rings. David looked around his apartment and took a deep breath.

The phone kept ringing. He counted ten rings. No answer. He hung up and sighed. David leaned back in his chair. The frustration was palpable.

David got up and went to his camera equipment. It was still all full of sand from the night before. Carefully, he blew the sand away and wiped the equipment with a small towel.

He watched the clock and the second hand seemed to drag its way around the dial. He thought he would give it ten minutes and try calling again.

He watched the big red second hand. It seemed like it just stopped. It moved ever so slowly.

David threw the towel over the clock so he wouldn't keep watching it.

"Dammmn it." he said aloud.

He gave the camera a thorough cleaning and as soon as he could get his mind off Misty, the time seemed to pass more quickly. He uncovered the clock. Fifteen minutes had passed.

He dialed.

"This is it," he said.

It rang.

It rang again.

A third time.

David was about to hang up when a voice came on.

"Yeah?" It was a sarcastic man's voice.

"Misty?" David said without thinking.

"Do I sound like Misty?" said the voice.

"Ah, no, I mean," said David flustered. "Is Misty there?"

"You gotta be joshing me. Who is this?"

"My name's David, I was given this number for Misty."

"Yeah, well whoever your queer friend is who did that is some kind of moron." The phone hung up abruptly.

David listened to it beep. Slowly, he set the phone in its cradle.

"Son of a biiiiitch!" he said with conviction.

He couldn't believe it.

He called all four numbers. None of them were right. He had Misty Adams on the beach and he let her get away.

"Idiot!" he said. Not that self-deprecation made him feel any better, but David was beside himself. How could he have fallen asleep without getting the number?

And why did she write that number on his face? Did she want to talk to him or was she just messing with him?

"Damn it, damn it, damn it," he

said.

He put his feet up on the small magazine table in front of his chair. He put the rotary phone in his lap and reached for the phone book.

Okay, he thought, maybe he wasn't calling the right exchange. He double checked the telephone exchange for Hollywood Hills. TA-ylor was correct. He ran his finger across the map in the phone book. There was GA-rland, and EL-wood and FR-anklin. All of those were surrounding TA-ylor. And then, outside that, there were others.

David picked up the receiver. Four possible numbers, three more possible exchanges, what would be so hard about making twelve more phone calls?

How about FR4-5551? David dialed instinctively. Okay, so it wouldn't be right, but he could keep trying.

He listened to the phone ring. One ring. Two rings...

"Hello?" came a woman's voice.

"Hi, is Misty there please?"

"Speaking."

David could hardly respond.

"Misty Adams?"

"Yes," returned an incredibly sexy voice.

"This is Misty Adams?"

"Yes it is."

"Hi, Misty, this is David."

"David?"

"Yes, David, you know from the beach?"

There was a little giggle in Misty's voice, "You're the boy from the beach!"

"Yes! David. I'm David from the beach."

"I thought you'd call before now," she teased.

"I did!" said David, "or I tried. I've been trying to call you all morning."

"So what was the problem? It's noon."

David looked at his clock. It wasn't that late.

"Well, not quite, but I had a little trouble with the number."

"So it took you that long to look in the mirror?"

"No," said David. "I got the number, but you didn't give the exchange."

"Oh, sorry. I thought everybody knew where I lived."

"Well, yeah, I do, but...."

"So what did you need me to write the exchange for?"

"I called TA-ylor."

Misty laughed.

"No, no. It's FR-anklin."

"Yeah, I know, but I thought..."

"Oh, you called the mansion. The mansion is in TA-ylor. I don't live there. The house is just too big. It's too lonely."

"I thought..."

"No, I have another house. It's a lot smaller. Too many people try to meet me at the mansion. I don't even hardly go over there anymore except to pick up clothes or shoes."

"You have a lot of shoes?"

"Yes," she laughed. "I have a whole lot of shoes. You know a nice pair of high heels are a girl's best friend."

"Why is that exactly?"

"You ever see a girl with amazing legs?"

Look For Me

"Yes."

"It's because of the shoes."

"I guess you're right," said David smiling to himself.

"What did we do last night?"

"What?"

"I know what we did, I just want to hear your version of it," said Misty.

"What do you mean?" asked David.

"Tell me what we did," insisted Misty.

"We didn't do anything. I don't know what you mean."

"So why are you calling me?"

"You gave me your number."

"Why did I do that?" asked Misty.

"I don't know."

"We must have done something. So tell me what we did."

"Well," said David, "we met on the beach and we introduced ourselves and you invited me to go skinny dipping with you."

"And?"

"And, so I did," said David.

"With your clothes on?" asked Misty.

"No. I took my clothes off."

"Why?"

"What do you mean, why? Because you had your clothes off."

"That's what I thought," said Misty.

"Well, you invited me."

"Anything else?"

"Ah, well, we laid on the beach and talked."

"Together?" asked Misty.

"What do you mean? Of course, together. We weren't talking to ourselves."

"I was drunk," said Misty.

"I know," responded David. "That's okay."

"I'm not apologizing. I'm just telling the truth."

"Okay, I understand."

"Did we do anything else?" asked Misty.

"You don't remember?"

"Yes, I remember everything. I just want to know what you remember."

"You don't remember, do you?" asked David.

"You were pretty tricky to get my phone number."

"You gave it to me," said David.

"Did you ask for it?"

"No."

"You know men ask for my phone number all the time."

"I'm not surprised."

"You didn't ask for it?"

"No."

"Then why did I give it to you?"

"I don't know, you just did," said David.

"I never give my phone number to men who make a pass at me," said Misty.

"I didn't make a pass at you."

"Oh, so that's it. You're the only nice guy in Los Angeles."

"I've been called a gentleman before."

"You are a gentleman. You're on the beach skinny dipping with Misty Adams and you don't make a move on her. That's pretty unusual."

"I'm sorry."

"Don't be sorry. I like that. All men want from me is sex. Don't get me wrong. I like sex. But I'm not easy."

David was a little surprised to hear Misty talking so frankly about a subject seldom discussed.

"No, I'm sure you are not."

"You would have had sex with me though wouldn't you, if you could?"

David was flabbergasted.

"Ah..."

"Don't lie. Tell me the truth."

"I, ah. Look, I just met you."

"So you are a nice guy. That's something original."

"Thank you. I think."

There was a pause on the telephone. David wasn't sure what to think. The talk had made him a little aroused.

"So tell me, what did you say your name was?" asked Misty.

"You seem to have trouble with that."

"What?"

"My name."

"Oh, I'm sorry. There are so many names. I don't remember them all. But I want to remember yours. You're different."

"My name is David."

"David. That's a handsome name and as I remember, you're a handsome boy. Let me ask you..."

"I want to ask you..." said David, saying the exact same thing as Misty. They both laughed.

"Go ahead," said Misty.

"No, you," said David.

"You start," insisted Misty.

"Well, I was just going to ask you. You remember from last night that I'm a photographer, right?"

There was no reply immediately.

"Misty?" asked David.

"I'm a photographer. And I had this idea..."

"Are you paparazzi?"

"No," said David sternly. "No, I told you that last night. I don't run with that crowd. I'm a nature photographer."

"Nature?"

"Yeah, you know, sunsets and landscapes. I photograph natural beauty."

"Like me?" asked Misty.

"Like you, that's it. You are the most beautiful girl in the world."

"No I'm not. I'm pretty, but I'm not beautiful."

"People seem to think that you are."

"That's because they don't know me," she said.

"That's why I'm here. That's my idea. I want to photograph the real you. I want to show the world the real Misty Adams."

There was a silence on the phone.

"Misty?" asked David.

"You're different, David."

"Thanks."

"You know how many photographers want to take my picture and I don't give them the time of day?"

"Yes."

"But you're different. I think you're sincere. I think you really do

want to get to know me for who I am
and not for the image I've become."

"That's right," said David.
"That's exactly right."

There was another silence.

"Okay, David, Different David,
I'll do it."

David's mind raced. He couldn't
believe his ears.

"That's great," said David.

The two chatted another twenty
minutes. A date was arranged and
Misty agreed to put it on her calendar.
David wanted to shoot a documentary
of the photo shoot but Misty refused
that. Stills only, that was the deal.
They would meet at 5 pm in three days.
David said he would have a studio set
up with lights and that they could try a
couple of things and that they could
talk and he would make notes for an article to go with the pictures. Misty
made him agree that she had right of
refusal on any of the pictures she didn't
like. If she didn't like something, it
would not be published.

David half argued the point,

sticking up for his artistic integrity, but, he gave in. After all, this was Misty Adams. This was a huge star. This was a woman who could pick any photographer she wanted, and had, and could fire anybody at the drop of a hat.

When he hung up the phone, David was high. There is no question if he died that moment, he would have been satisfied. Just getting to talk to Misty was incredible and the very thought of actually photographing her was unprecedented.

The next couple of days went by in a blur. David had no place to photograph Misty. She did not want to do it outdoors and so he had to have a place inside that was suitable. His apartment was too small. She didn't want to do it at the mansion; said she hated the mansion. So he promised her a studio.

He found a place off Hollywood Boulevard and rented it for a week. It had a huge loft and while it was barely furnished, it had plenty of room.

He did not own the lights it

would take to set it up, so he rented those, too. Thank goodness there were places around town that did that sort of thing.

David also hired an assistant. He didn't want anything to go wrong and the man he hired had worked for him a time or two before. He was reliable, and could adjust lights and change film.

David normally used a 35mm camera, but for this he thought he'd use that and a Hasselblad large format camera. The Hasselblad was something he bought second hand and didn't use much because he was more comfortable with the 35, but, this was Misty Adams. He had best be prepared for anything.

On the day Misty was to be photographed, David called about noon and spoke to her. All was set, he told her, and she said she'd be ready.

David kept pinching himself to see if he was still alive.

He had planned so long for this

but was not really prepared. He was excited, and nervous and so he arrived early at his makeshift studio and checked and rechecked his equipment. He was going to wrap Misty in some bright red or blue cloth and use a fan to blow her hair. That would be one set-up. Then, he had a couch brought in that he thought she could lounge on for some more poses.

David scrimmed the lights to give a soft appearance and covered the floor with paper to hide the old wooden boards. If he pumped out the light the paper would reflect and make a surreal appearance. With Misty in that mix, her stunning beauty could be captured. He hoped.

You never know about pictures, David thought. You just can't ever tell up front. You plan and you think and you figure and you calculate, but you just don't know until the model arrives.

David chilled a bottle of wine.

He figured that would make it easier. He knew Misty drank wine, but he didn't think to ask her what kind.

So, he picked a red wine. The label said something about strawberries but he didn't really know wine, so he selected it because it sounded delicious. It would go with Misty's lips, he thought. And, he bought some strawberries at the market. Models don't like to eat when they are modeling, but David thought it would be a nice touch. She wouldn't have to eat them, but if she wanted to, she could.

By 4 pm he was all set. His assistant took a chair and they reviewed the plans. Everything was perfect.

By 5 pm David paced the floor. Misty was due and he looked out the window to see if she was pulling up. He gave her explicit instructions on how to find the place and she said that her driver could get her there.

At 6 pm David was pretty anxious. Most of the ice had melted and he sent his helper out to get more. He had already eaten most of the strawberries.

When 7 pm arrived David's nerves were pretty much raw.

Misty Adams was true to her

reputation, that was for sure. Two hours late is pretty late.

David began to think maybe she wasn't coming. There was no phone in the room so he couldn't call and he didn't dare leave to find a telephone.

David sat down and took a couple of pictures of himself waiting.

Maybe his story would end up being the day he almost photographed Misty Adams.

At 7:30 pm David started getting depressed. Had she stood him up? Was she just leading him along on the phone? Did she get nervous and decide not to do the photo shoot?

Then there was a rap on the door.

David shot out of the chair like an excited poodle.

He bumped into his assistant on his way over to the door.

He opened it.

Misty stood there with her driver just behind.

She was dazzling. She had put her long blonde hair up. A couple of strands dangled on her cheek. David could not believe his eyes. What he saw then and there was the legend, and not at all the same woman he had met on the beach. His mouth hung open a little and he didn't speak.

"Well, are you going to invite me in, Different David?" asked Misty.

"Yes, yes, please come in," he said.

David opened the door wider and Misty walked by. Her perfume hit him like a million blossoms. David held his hand out to the driver.

"I'm David," he said.

"Drake," said the driver as he shook David's hand.

David followed Misty inside.

"This is my assistant, William." Drake shook his hand.

William hurried over to turn on the lights.

David turned to him, "Not yet, give us a few minutes."

Misty was wearing a light wrap. She placed it on the couch.

"I've seen better studios," she

said.

David tried to apologize, but before he could say anything, Misty looked him directly in the eyes.

"But I've never seen a cuter photographer."

David breathed a sigh of relief.

"So what do you have in mind?" asked Misty.

"Well," David began, "I thought we'd start by having you wrap in some colorful fabrics, something with a lot of tonal range. Start with red, maybe add some blue."

Misty looked at him with anticipation.

"Oh," said David as he fumbled with the cloth to show her, "these."

Misty looked at them. She touched them.

"That might work," she said.

David held his hand out toward the couch.

"Would you like to sit a minute?"

Misty looked at the couch. "Oh, what a beautiful couch. This is just superb. Look at this ornate carving. I love this couch."

She turned to Drake quickly. "I want to buy this couch." She turned back. "David, is this yours?"

"No," he said. "I rented this flat and the couch for the studio."

Misty spun around to Drake again. "Find out who owns this incredible couch and offer to buy it. It is a very special couch." She ran her hands across the wood. The wine was sitting on a small table nearby. Misty noticed it.

"Ohhh, you brought some wine."

"Yes, would you like some?" asked David.

Misty smiled. "Thank you, Different David."

David twisted out the cork and poured Misty a glass.

She took it immediately and pressed it to her lips.

"Oh, this is wonderful. What is this?"

"Ah, I, ah,..." David fumbled with the label.

Misty put her hand on his to stop

him.

"Don't tell me. I'll remember it as David's wine."

David smiled.

"So, did you have any trouble finding this place?" David asked. David offered her strawberries and she took one but waved the others off.

"Aren't you going to have some wine?" asked Misty ignoring the question.

"Well, I don't ah, I don't. Sure." David poured a little into another glass and tasted it.

"Isn't it good?" asked Misty.

"Yes, this tastes like strawberries."

"I knooow," said Misty, holding her glass over toward David so he could add some more out of the bottle even though her glass was still mostly full.

"Do you want to sit?"

"No, David, I think I just want to look around a little."

Misty twirled as if she was in a huge studio. It was very modest but Misty took it all in. She breathed in, sipped, looked around.

David watched her with a smile on his face. He had never seen a model like this one. She seemed so alive, so happy to be there, as if it was the most important thing ever. No wonder the world loved her. She loved the world.

Misty walked over to the window and gazed out as she sipped her wine.

David didn't know what to say, so he didn't say anything.

Misty turned abruptly and looked him directly in the eye.

"What do you think of me, David?"

Without hesitation, David stepped toward her. "You're the most gorgeous woman I've ever seen."

"Liar," Misty said with a little tease.

"You look incredible."

Drake and William stood off to the side but they each gave the other a 'can you believe this?' glance.

"I like you, David. You're different."

"How am I different?"

"I don't know, you just are."

David walked over toward a chair near the window and pulled it out from the wall a little.

"Mind if I sit down?"

Misty looked at him.

"Would you pour me a little more of that wonderful wine?"

David retrieved the bottle.

Misty curiously poked around in David's open camera bag. David watched her carefully. That wasn't a normal thing for a model to do, but this was Misty Adams, so he let her do as she pleased.

She pulled a little camera out of the bag. It was an old antique David bought on his way out to California. He kept it around just because it was made in 1916.

"What's this?" she asked.

"Oh, just an old camera." David reached for it and Misty handed it to him. He popped open the bellows and pointed it at Misty. She posed. David saw his own reflection in the window juxtaposed next to Misty. He clicked the shutter.

"Well that doesn't sound like very much," said Misty.

"I don't even know if it works. I haven't even developed the film that's in it."

Misty smiled.

"How do you want me to use that cloth?" asked Misty.

"Ah," said David, "I thought you could just wrap it around like clothing. That would be your clothing. And we could have one end come up in one direction and the other end out back toward the floor."

"As if I'm considering colors from a dress maker?" asked Misty.

"Right," said David. "That's right."

"I love the idea." Misty looked around the room. "Where do you want me to change?"

"This is just a one room apartment," said David, "but I thought you could change over in the bathroom. Will that be all right?"

"I could change right here," said

Misty seductively.

"Well, ah..."

"You're blushing." David did blush when she said that. It was all so familiar, so friendly, as if he had known her for a long time.

"Drake," said Misty looking at her driver. "I think you two need to go take a long drive. I want to be alone with this boy."

"Yes ma'am," said Drake immediately.

William looked at David and used his shoulders to question the request. David used his head to indicate William should go with Drake.

Misty walked toward the bathroom.

"Would you bring me my wardrobe, please, sire?" said Misty with a bit of a playful command.

David followed her with several bolts of cloth.

Misty reached back to unzip her form-fitted dress. She fumbled a bit as she stood in the bathroom doorway.

"Would you help me, please?" she

asked.

Timidly, David reached over and started the zipper down where she could better grasp it.

"That's all?" she asked with a smile.

"I think you can..."

"Suppose I want a little more help?" asked Misty, interrupting.

David zipped the dress down further revealing Misty's bra. Her skin was tanned but below the bra it was milky white.

David hesitated.

"Go ahead," said Misty.

"I, thought..."

"Go ahead, Different David. You've already seen me naked."

"At the beach," said David quietly.

"We've been skinny dipping together," said Misty with a giggle.

"Well it was pretty dark."

"What's darkness except the absence of sun?" asked Misty.

David nodded his head nervously.

"Yes, I suppose you are right."

David zipped the dress all the way down to her bottom.

"That's better," she said as she quickly took the cloth out of David's hand and pushed him out of the doorway with the tip of her fingers.

David backed up with surprise.

Misty laughed as she slowly closed the door looking directly at David's eyes.

Wow, thought David, this woman is full of surprises. He couldn't help but feel she had him in the palm of her hand. He walked away from the bathroom with a shake to his head. She arrived late, she kicked everybody out, she teased him and then disappeared behind the door.

David poured himself some more wine and finished it rather quickly. He felt warmth in his head. He considered himself to be a good photographer, but this shoot was going to be a challenge. He was totally off his game and in her court.

David looked around the room.

Everything was set. He sat down to wait. But then about the time he was settled, the bathroom swung open and out stepped Misty.

"Ta-da!" she said as she held one hand low and another in the air.

Instinctively David clapped.

"Incredible!"

"Do you like it?"

"Yes, yes I do," said David nodding his head.

Misty waltzed over toward David and did a little spin. She had used blue and yellow in a combination wrap. He wondered how she was able to do it, but then thought, this is a very talented woman.

Misty smiled. "I thought you would like it, sir." Misty looked around the room. "Where's my wine?"

"Oh," said David as he jumped up. He retrieved her glass, which was almost empty, and handed it to her.

"That's it?" asked Misty.

David got the bottle and poured the glass full. There wasn't much left in the bottle.

Look For Me

Misty sipped the wine.

"What a great year," she said. "It's 1956!"

David smiled and clinked his glass to hers.

"To 1956, a great year!"

Misty swallowed a little deeper. There was still some wine in her glass but David poured the remainder from the bottle into it. Misty sipped a little more. She looked around.

"Where do you want me? Where David, Different David?"

David turned on the lights one-by-one.

"I was thinking you could stand over here in the light by the fan and we'll work on this side over here."

Misty looked.

"Okay, I can do that."

David got his camera and walked over to a spot in front of Misty.

Without instruction, Misty struck a pose.

"That's excellent," said David.

"Thank you Different David," she said.

"Oh," said David, reaching to take her glass from her.

"Shoot some with me holding this wine, David's wine," she suggested.

David took a couple of shots as Misty posed first one way and then another, arm over her head, hand holding the glass near her hip.

David moved to get additional angles as Misty slowly turned to look at him over her shoulder. As she moved, David made pictures, slowly at first, a little faster as they proceeded.

Misty moved again and the cloth wrap came loose at the shoulder and slipped down to her nipples and showed some of her breast. Misty laughed but did not cover herself.

David stood up straight and stopped taking pictures.

"Go ahead, Different David, you wanted to see the real Misty Adams."

"You sure?"

"Why not?" asked Misty. "It's natural. I feel better without clothes."

Carefully, David moved in and framed what looked to him like a beautiful picture. He had never seen anything that striking through his lens. He took a photograph. He hesitated.

"That's it?" asked Misty.

David felt aroused. He was a little embarrassed, but he tried to hide by turning sideways to take the next picture.

He looked through the lens again and as Misty struck the perfect pose he released the shutter.

It was incredible. She was incredible. She was the perfect female form. David took another picture as Misty started to wiggle her hips. David felt the moisture leave his mouth and he could feel the camera shake a little.

"You're so pretty."

"Thank you," said Misty softly. She gazed at him. David couldn't help but look in her eyes and be mesmerized. It was like she was putting him into a trance.

He stopped taking pictures again and the two looked at each other for a few seconds.

Then, they both started to speak

at the same time.

"Do you want to..." said David.

"David, I..." said Misty.

They both laughed.

"Go ahead," said David.

"No, you," replied Misty.

"I was going to ask, would you like to move over to the couch?" asked David.

"I was going to suggest that very thing," said Misty.

Misty held the cloth up to her breasts and walked over to the couch. David watched her.

"Do you have any more wine?"

David retrieved the bottle and poured a couple of drops into Misty's glass.

"Ah, yes," he said after a silence. "But it's not cold."

"Well lucky for us," she said, "I'm Irish."

"So am I," said David.

"Well that's it, then," said Misty. "That's why I like you."

David went to his camera bags he had left beside the window. He pulled out a second bottle of wine.

"I didn't know if you'd like it so I didn't chill it."

"That's quite all right, Different David."

David removed the cork as Misty adjusted the cloth she had wrapped around her.

David poured her another glass.

"You know something," said Misty, "I don't like this cloth anymore."

"Why not?" asked David a little surprised.

"It's cheap."

"I'm sorry," said David.

"But I'm not."

"I'm really sorry, I didn't mean to imply..."

"No, don't worry about it," said Misty. "I just won't wear it."

David felt the blood rush inside his body.

"Do you have a sheet?" asked Misty.

"Yes, I think, I think there's some linens over here," said David as he headed to a cabinet beside the bathroom. While he had been waiting for her to arrive he had thoroughly searched the place to kill time. He located a stack of sheets and pulled out a very pretty white one. He held it up.

"That's perfect," said Misty. "Bring it here."

David walked it over to her.

"Now go, turn around," said Misty as she swished him with her hand.

She opened the sheet and unwrapped the colored cloth from her body. She had nothing on underneath. David got a glimpse of her in the reflection in the window. She waved the sheet in the air to spread it and let it fly down on top of her. The colored cloth was draped on the couch, partly on the floor, partly under her.

"Okay, turn around," said Misty.

David looked at her with approval.

"Nice," he said.

"Nice?" said Misty.

"No, I mean, it looks great. You, you look great."

"Don't disappoint me Mr. Photographer. If you lie to me I'll know because I've been lied to before," she said pointedly.

"I like it," said David as he nodded his head. "Except, we need to take the colors out and just use the white."

"Oh, yeah," she said as she wiggled and pulled the colored cloth out from under her body. David got a little peek at her as she did.

He looked around and located his camera. He didn't even remember ever setting it down. Misty accidently knocked her wine glass over. It didn't have much wine in it but David grabbed another linen and sopped up the spill.

"I would have just left it," said Misty. "You don't live here, do you?"

"No," said David.

"Then give the landlord something to gossip about. We'll leave my bra in the bathroom, too."

David laughed and shook his head.

"You're very funny," he said.

"I'm not trying to be funny,"

smiled Misty, "I'm trying to be me."

"Well, that would be you," said David. He reached out and adjusted one of the cushions on the couch and fussed a little with the sheet.

"What do you think of me now, Different David?"

"I think you're great. Sensational," said David.

"How about sensual?" asked Misty.

"That, too," answered David.

David stepped back and looked through the lens of the camera.

"What should I do?" asked Misty.

"You're already doing it," said David in return. He snapped a picture. Misty moved. He took another. She moved again.

David was amazed at how smooth and natural she was in front of the camera. It was if she was making love to it. Or maybe she was making love to him, through it, he wasn't sure. He certainly felt it and he certainly took a lot of frames.

He stood, he knelt, he climbed up

on the loft and shot down as she teased him through the sheet. He could see through the sheet, barely, but that made the photos more arresting and Misty sensed that he was loving it.

Finally, as David stopped to rewind the film and load another roll, Misty reached her arm toward him and beckoned him with her fingers.

"Why don't you come join me under this sheet?" she asked.

David could hardly stick the next roll of film in the camera.

He didn't know what to say, so he stumbled over his words.

"I, ah, um, I..."

"Come on Different David, it's just the two of us," said Misty softly.

"But we need the pictures. Let's finish the pictures."

Misty laughed lightly.

"You are so different!"

"I, ah,..."

"You can't talk, David. You're speechless," said Misty as though she was proud of the way she made him lose composure.

"Take your pictures, handsome, you sweet little darling. But you don't know what you are missing."

"Yeah, I think I do," said David.

He focused the camera and took a few more pictures. Misty moved with creative instinct that made every frame good. No, it wasn't good. It was fantastic. Every picture was brilliant. Each time the shutter snapped, David felt as though a piece of time was frozen, as if history was being captured.

He wanted to stop and cuddle with her, or do whatever she wanted to do under that sheet, but he didn't dare. The pictures, the pictures. That's all he could think. Concentrate on the pictures.

"I can see you are thinking about me," said Misty, looking at his pants.

David smiled.

"Oh, I'm thinking about you. I'm thinking about how I am going to be needing to take a really cold shower when this is done."

Misty smiled with a wide grin. She liked that.

The photo session went on another half hour or so until Misty announced she was tired. They stopped. Misty leaned back on the couch and David placed his camera on the floor and stretched out beside the couch. He kicked his shoes off.

They talked. They shared memories and they shared dreams and they laughed. Misty finished her wine. David left a little in his glass.

She dressed and when David walked her to the door he could see the limousine was parked across the street. Drake and William were sitting on the hood. Who knows what they talked about or how bored they must have been while waiting all that time.

David walked Misty to the car and it was agreed they'd meet again in three days to review the photos.

And then Misty drove off.

David felt strange. He did not want her to leave. He could not believe what had just happened and seeing her go was a letdown. William packed up the equipment while David sat watching him.

"William," said David eventually, "I'm sorry you didn't get to stay. Misty Adams just seduced my camera, and in these rolls of film is so much energy I just can't describe it. It's definitely a cold shower day."

The three days passed quickly. David had all the film processed. He would have gotten proof sheets but Misty insisted he make only negatives and bring only negatives. She had made it clear all along that nothing from the session would be used without her approval.

It was an unusual request. In fact, it just wasn't done. Photographers always have final say in which pictures are used and which are not. Models never get to choose. Models seldom even get to see the pictures until they are published.

But this was Misty Adams. This was a big star. This was a lady who had been photographed thousands of times by hundreds of photographers. And she told David up front--no pictures at all if she didn't get to determine which would be used and which would not be used.

David had gotten a private room in a little restaurant that nobody knew. Misty was ushered in through the back door and management agreed to keep the meeting quiet.

When she arrived David was struck by something very different about Misty. She was just as pretty. She was a knockout. But she was all business. She was not playful as he had seen before. She was not prone to tease him. She was like a completely different person.

She was very pleasant, said "hello" and called David "Different David"--which he liked. But she was distant, too.

They sat on the same side of the table with the box of negatives in front of them.

The waiter came in and they ordered drinks and promised to eat a little something later.

"So how do they look?" asked

Misty.

David slowly opened the box and pulled out the first set.

Misty studied them very carefully, looking first at one and then another. She'd say, "yes, yes," as she pulled the negatives gently through her hands. But David noticed sometimes she'd just look and say nothing. A time or two she'd say, "I like this one." A couple of times she laughed out loud as pictures depicted her clowning, or reminded her of how she made him fumble. Misty leaned close to David and he could feel the warmth of her breast on his shoulder.

She looked at almost all of the negatives and then opened her handbag and pulled out a pair of scissors.

David was puzzled.

Misty held a strip of negatives up to the light.

"Yes, yes..."

Then she stopped, squinted a little and before David knew what she was doing, she cut a negative right through the middle.

David was startled, shocked, taken aback. He could not believe what he just witnessed.

"What are you doing?" he asked.

She cut another one.

"I don't like this one," she said.

David could almost feel a tear welling up in his eye. He had gone through the negatives carefully before the meeting and they were good. They were really good.

"Why are you cutting these?" he asked.

"I don't like them and I don't want you to use them."

David did not know what to say. It was as if someone had just run over his dog and killed his mother at the same time.

He watched as Misty went through the rest of the box. On the table, pieces of what once were great pictures, turned now to memories. Misty Adams cut negatives she didn't want the public to see and that was that.

She started to cut one of the

nearly barebreasted pictures and David's heart fell into his diaphragm. Then she looked over at David and smiled.

"I'll let you keep that one," she said, "because you're such a gentleman. You're different and so you deserve to have that one."

David's emotions were on edge. This woman made him crazy. He could not believe what was happening but he was so happy that it was.

They ate dinner after that and when it was all done Misty was on her way. Drake waited outside and off they went.

David went back to his place with a box full of negatives and an experience that would never be topped.

Chapter 9

1957
Hollywood, California

The pictures from the Misty Adams session were brilliant. David had them published in *Star Life* magazine along with a lengthy and intimate article. David gave a perspective on the star that had not been appreciated before. America loved her and the article humanized her and helped people understand the pressures of stardom and the perfection to which she held herself when acting.

The country was ready to see more of Misty Adams and letters flooded into the studio offices in Hollywood. Her studio responded with a

telephone call that resulted in a re-
union between Misty and her director.
The picture she had started more than
a year and half before was taken out of
mothballs and finished.

It was difficult but spectacular
work. Misty Adams was not just another headliner. She was the whole
production, and the emotion and sensi-
tivity she put on screen, were unprecedented.

David visited her on the set quite
a bit. She called him and sent Drake to
pick him up. He was only too happy to
oblige and was given a key to her
trailer.

Inside the trailer David got to
know a very different girl.

She was tough on the outside,
constantly making demands of the
crew, being difficult, lashing out and
moody. Behind that closed door,
though, she was insecure, and fearful
and in constant need of reassurance.
And then there were the prescription
medications. She had a whole array of
pills--some to help her sleep, some to

wake her up, some that made her feel small, some that made her feel nothing at all. And alcohol, there was always alcohol. She loved wine and drank it like water. But when she was really nervous about something, uncertain about a scene, the liquor was hard.

She didn't sip her drinks, she gulped them. She was often sick, nauseous and she frequently threw up. That's why she was constantly late. Nobody knew that about her. She couldn't get to the set call on time because she was perpetually nervous and depressed and in pain, yet sometimes, euphoric and gregarious. It was unpredictable from day to day.

David knew. David saw it. And David's heart went out to her. She was magnetic despite the problems, and she was needy and he wanted to help her. But the drug cocktail she was consuming was working on her in a bad way. The sweet Misty was there, but it was hard to find. David tried to encourage her to back off from the drugs, but she would have nothing of it. She would explode at him only to feel remorse a half hour later and forgive him.

"What is wrong with me, David?" she would ask.

"I don't know" he said, as he cuddled her on the bench seat in her trailer.

"Why can't I feel normal? Why am I so confused?"

David rubbed her shoulder. He had no idea. He knew the drugs and the alcohol were making it worse. He knew that these things were not the answer to her happiness. But she was addicted. She was so conditioned to put something in her mouth to try to feel better that she did it all and mixed it and there wasn't a moment where she was truly clearheaded.

The doctor assigned to her was no help. The studio paid him and his goal was to keep her functioning to the end of the picture. They really didn't care what happened to Misty Adams as long as she finished the picture. *The picture, the picture.* That's all they cared about.

In quiet moments she told David about all the men who had abused her in the past, how she hated them and would never forgive them. David thought that that was why she enjoyed controlling men. It was a form of psychological payback. Men were drawn to her but she didn't like them. But she did like David because he was sensitive and caring and gentle, and he listened. He was probably the only one who truly listened to her. And he would stroke her hand when she talked and she loved that.

David had never dreamed that he would get close to Misty Adams. His original plan was to photograph her, help her stage a comeback and boost his own career. But he hadn't done any real work since she called him to the set. He got the inquiries. There were all kinds of stars and wannabe stars who wanted David Ross to do a photo session. They all believed that he was the one who saved the Misty Adams career, and with that reputation his work could launch anybody.

But David wasn't interested. He was too emotionally attached to Misty and too intent on seeing her through to the end of the job and beyond.

His camera was ever present but seldom used. Misty didn't want him to take pictures of her except when she was in the mood and that was so unpredictable that David just held on to the idea that they would someday do more work together. But first, he had to get her through the present job.

There was a rap on the trailer door.

"Half hour, Miss Adams," came the voice of a production assistant with the dubious job of getting her out of her trailer and to call on time.

It was a game with the studio. If they thought she would be needed in two hours, they started banging on her door telling her she had thirty minutes a couple of hours before they really needed her. She knew it and didn't care. She was not about to walk through that door until she was composed and good and ready.

David felt the stress and had taken to drinking some of Misty's liquor. He didn't drink much, but he drank more with her than at any other time in his life.

"We're going to need to get you ready," said David finally.

"I don't want to act today."

"Why? You know the lines, we practiced them last night."

"What day is it?" asked Misty.

"I don't know," said David, "I think it's Wednesday or Thursday."

"We've worked all week. Tell them we don't work on the weekend."

"It isn't the weekend," said David.

Misty looked up at David.

"Do you love me, David?"

"Yes I do," said David.

"Do you really love me?"

"Yes, you know that."

"I want to hear you say it."

"I love you, Misty."

Misty turned her head and placed it on David's chest. She listened to his breathing.

"Let's take the day off and go to the beach," she said with a high note.

"You know we can't do that."

Misty abruptly pushed away from David.

"Misty," said David, "it's just a couple of more weeks, then we will go on a long vacation."

"Promise?"

"I promise."

Sometimes that was all it took to get Misty out of her rut, at least for the day, or the hour. She would go out into the daylight and steal every scene. She would frustrate and amaze the crew. She didn't always follow the lines. A lot of times she messed the lines up completely. But that didn't matter. She became the character and she was better at it than the writer had intended.

The picture eventually did get in the can and the studio wrapped the production. It was cut and mastered and publicized and David was hired to shoot the movie poster and associated stills.

It wasn't news around town that David was the new Misty Adams love interest. The tabloids followed them and the paparazzi tried to get pictures of them together.

It was exciting. Misty was fun when she was out of her funk and David was quite the gentleman. He was handsome and young and the fans adored the couple.

When the premier finally arrived, it was a red carpet event to end all such events. The studio put out a lot of money to sell this as the biggest picture of the year and even before anybody had seen it, there was Oscar talk.

David couldn't believe the whirlwind of publicity leading up to the premier and the photographers and the flash bulbs and the fans and studio executives. It was incredible to be on Misty's arm.

She was stunning, dressed in a full length sequin dress with bare shoulders. She was drunk, as usual, but somehow people didn't fully realize it. David had no idea how she continued to function, but she did.

The picture was wonderful, the after party went on all night, even though Misty had long since fallen asleep, or passed out, however it really was.

Drake got them home--to the mansion. Misty didn't mind the mansion when David was there. It wasn't lonely with him there, she told him. In fact, David had his own room and while they were occasional lovers, he didn't sleep with her on a regular basis.

Misty liked to spread out on her own bed and sleep well into the afternoon. She had a huge round bed with satin sheets and plenty of pillows. She always kept the drapes drawn to keep out the light.

A week passed and they went on vacation, to Hawaii. Two weeks there, another few days in Tahiti and then back home. The trip made all the papers.

It was when they arrived back home that all the glitz and glamor faded and Misty escalated her pills and her alcohol use.

David tried to talk her out of it, but that just made it worse. She was her own woman. She was not about to be told what to do and even though David did it out of love, she resented him when he tried to slow down the drugs and the alcohol.

It all got to David after awhile and they spent less and less time with each other. David did love her, which is probably why it became so hard for him. He could see her behavior leading her to a brick wall, and fast.

"Misty, let's go for a drive," he said one afternoon. She was still in her nightgown, still in bed. "Misty?"

David tapped on the door and entered her room.

She looked awful. Her eyes seemed clouded and the circles around them were more pronounced than usual. She had lost a lot of weight and did not look well at all.

"Misty, let's get you cleaned up and go for a drive. It's such a pretty day."

"I hate the light," she said.

"Come on, let me help you." David opened a curtain and Misty screeched, so he closed it. He went over to the bed and sat next to her.

"Come on, let me help you into the shower."

"I have a headache," she complained.

"I know, I'll get you an aspirin."

"An aspirin is not what I need. Where's my medicine?"

Misty fumbled on the night stand to find a bottle of pills. She took two or three and swallowed them with what was left of a glass of bourbon.

"Now that's really going to help," David said snidely.

"What the hell do you care for?" Misty exploded. "You're not the one with the stupid headache!"

David tried to rub her head but she pushed his hand away.

"Get away from me."

"Misty, I'm just trying to help you. How can you choose a life of misery over me?"

"You can help me by shutting the hell up!"

David breathed out and slowly stood up. This was not the first time she had treated him that way. Indeed, it was pretty much every time she had a hangover, which was practically every day.

David stood and looked at her crumpled in the bed. How could a woman with such talent and so much kindness to give the world, be so turned in on herself? David had no idea what to do. He was in love with her and she had told him that she was in love with him. But at times it seemed like she hated him and at times like this he certainly didn't feel affectionate toward her. But then he remembered one time she called him up when she was out drunk somewhere and she said, "I just called to tell you I love you." Another time they had had a disagreement and she told him over the phone, "I've been thinking about you all day. I was looking for a reason to hate you, but I could-

n't find one. I'm in love with you."
Other times she had told him, "You're
everything I want in a man."

David watched Misty breathing
slowly on the bed. Maybe she would go
back to sleep. It was heart-wrenching
to see what she had become. And as for
David, he felt as if she loved the drugs
more than him. It was like competing
with Jesus. You can't win that one.

"Screw the drugs," said David finally.

"What?" said Misty softly.

"Screw your drugs," repeated
David. "Screw your drugs. I don't even
know who you are. One minute you're
sweet and lovable and the next minute
you are hateful and mean. I don't know
who I'm talking to half the time."

"My head hurts," she moaned.

"I'm sorry about your head,
Misty. Did you ever once think that you
are doing this to yourself? There is no
way a body can tolerate the amount of
pills you take or the alcohol you flush
them down with. I don't even know
how you are walking around. I do love

you. I really do. But sometimes I can't stand the way you act. I want to help you. I want to work with you. I want you to be happy. But you won't let me. You just drive me away."

Misty rolled over to look at David.

"You're different, David," she said.

"Oh, God," said David. "I mean it this time. I mean it, Misty. You came back from this same kind of thing, you were nominated for an Academy because of your brilliant acting. But now you're back into this. And don't think I don't know how you sneak out at night. You don't think I hear Drake when he pulls out and you're gone for half the night?"

"What business is it of yours?" snapped Misty.

"I guess it's not, Misty. I guess it is none of my business. You're so self-destructive it is beyond description. Why won't you let me help you? Of course I can't help you if you don't want help. Do you know that? Do you understand that?" David walked toward the door. "If you don't want me here, all you have to do is say so."

"I do want you here," said Misty. "I need you here. You saved my life."

David looked down at the floor.

He had heard that before. He had had this very same conversation a dozen times.

"And so? Nothing ever changes," he said.

"Why should I change? I'm Misty Adams."

David shook his head.

"And that's the problem. You don't know who you really are anymore. I don't even know who you are. You've crawled inside a bottle and you are nothing but the drugs you take. That's who you've become. And if you don't stop, you won't know me and you won't know the real you."

David stepped through the door. "I'm going to go take some pictures at the coast. You're welcome to go with me. Or get Drake to bring you out. *Look for me. I will find you.*" David hesitated. "Another time, another place," he whispered.

"I love you," said Misty softly. David did not respond. He saw that she was not getting up, so he left her. It would be just another typical day. She'd sleep until she got about half sober and then she'd get up and start drinking and downing pills again until she passed out. Up all night, sleep all day, complain of pain. Depressed. Tomorrow would be exactly the same thing. And this was the girl that he told himself he was meant to be with. It was crazy.

David got his camera gear and drove his own car out the drive. Misty did not get up when he left.

David waved at Drake as he drove down the long drive. Drake polished the limo.

David drove down the coastal highway along the beach, to a place he knew where the cliffs overlooked the ocean. Way down below was the sand, but up high you could see for miles and it felt as though you were in the clouds with the seagulls.

David loved the spot and sat for awhile just taking it all in. It was spectacular. The ocean smelled so fresh and the breeze jostled his hair. He felt so alive, and yet, so lonely.

He remembered that first night he had seen Misty on the beach. She was beautiful. She was such a special human being. The camera loved her. The people loved her. He loved her. But she did not love herself. That was the problem. She did not love herself. She insisted on making herself numb. David always thought about her when he was away from her. He always wanted to be with her, except when the drugs were ruling her life. But for certain, he could not get her out of his mind. It was if they were destined to be together, destined to share lives together. And that made it all the more difficult to watch her hurting herself.

David took his tripod and walked out toward the cliff. It would be an incredible sunset. There were just enough clouds, and a nice breeze kept them moving across the sky. The air smelled so fresh and clean. David wished Misty was there. She would be the perfect subject in front of such a tremendous background.

David created a few pictures and watched silently as the sun disappeared into the ocean.

Drake was on his way home after having taken the limo out to get the oil changed. He tuned the radio.

"And repeating breaking news from the last hour. A tragic accident has occurred and the latest news is that celebrity photographer David Ross has been found dead at Topanga. Witnesses say they saw the photographer near the edge of the cliff apparently photograph-ing the scenery when the ground gave way. He was pronounced dead at the scene. Ross has been dating screen ac-tress Misty Adams since her long awaited return to the big screen..."

Drake's eyes watered and a lump welled up in his throat. He pressed hard on the accelerator to get back to

Misty. He knew that when she heard the news someone would have to be with her.

Drake knew the roads well and he knew exactly how hard he could push the limo and stay on the road.

As he neared the mansion, he noticed an unusual number of cars on the road and as he got closer to the drive he saw cars parked on both sides of the street. There were paparazzi photographers hurrying up the drive. Drake tried to pull into the drive with his limo. He honked. There was no way to go any further.

Then he looked toward the house and saw an ambulance. A group of men was rolling a stretcher out of the house toward the ambulance as the photographers ignited their flash bulbs. A policeman pushed them back.

Drake jogged up the drive to the stretcher.

A man held Drake back.

"What happened?" asked Drake.

"I don't know, somebody said drug overdose."

Drake stopped short. The blood rushed out of his head.

"She going to be okay?" someone asked.

"She's expired," said one of the men pushing the stretcher.

"Does she know about David Ross?" asked a man who just came up, having heard the news on the radio and driven over to Misty Adams to get her reaction, same as the others who were there.

"She's dead, man," said a voice.

"Dead?" asked another.

And so it was. David Ross accidently fell to his death and Misty Adams overdosed on drugs the same day. It was quite a story. The drug overdose was ruled accidental. Clumps of hill are always falling toward the ocean. Both of them should have known better. And both paid the price.

Chapter 10

October 24, 2008
Canyon Lake, Texas

Lauri pulled her lips away from Wallace's lips. She looked intently into his eyes and he into hers. That moment was locked in their memory and when it occurred, thoughts were triggered that they both remembered, together, simultaneously.

"Why did you do that?" asked Wallace.

"I feel like I knew you before," said Lauri.

"Before what?"

"Before now," returned Lauri.

"I don't understand," said Wallace.

Lauri leaned over and kissed him again. A rush of memories filled both their heads. Ever so slowly Lauri moved back.

"Do you see?" asked Lauri.

"I think so," said Wallace.

"*Look for me*," she said.

"*I will find you*," Wallace answered slowly.

A tear ran down Lauri's face.

"*Look for me*," she said.

"*I will find you*," replied Wallace again.

"Don't you see?"

"I do see," said Wallace. "I do see. Meallan?"

"Yes," she said slowly. "Yes, yes! Dub!"

Lauri grabbed Wallace and pulled him toward her. They kissed lovingly. Tears streamed down Lauri's face. Just then a distant cloud flashed and lightning lit the night sky. A mild thunder rumbled.

"I have found you. I looked everywhere," said Lauri. "And for so long."

"Me, too," said Wallace. "I can't believe this. Why do we know? How do we know this?"

"I don't care. We're finally together again. We're finally here."

Lauri raised Wallace's hand up to her face and placed his fingers on her cheek.

"This is real," she said softly.

The man in the cemetery who was about to kill himself hugged the woman who just happened to walk up that night as if he had not seen her in a thousand years. He held her so tightly they both thought their bodies would melt into one. Their lost souls had returned from a long journey of brief encounters and they were reunited in an aura of energy. They were soul mates, soul mates forever.

"*Look for me*," whispered Wallace softly.

"*I will find you*," smiled Lauri. "I *have* found you."

Genesis of a Story

By Douglas Kirk

The *Look For Me I Will Find You* series was conceived on October 24, 2008, in the very cemetery that forms the setting for the opening chapter. In the two years since the first book was written, and the production of the first mass market printing, the question has come up time and time again--how was the premise of this story conceived?

The best way to answer that is to describe how I wound up being in that 150 year old cemetery in the first place, after dark, with a battery operated flashlight that was losing its power.

It was not my first late evening visit to that cemetery. In fact, it was the fourth. It all started when I was looking to illustrate a Halloween article I was planning to publish in my newspaper. I wanted to illustrate a *Creep Tale*, a legend that is sometimes shared around the campfire or when people pass graveyards on old country roads after dark.

Look For Me

As the legend goes, a young couple was driving along a winding country road after their wedding. They left the reception perhaps a little tipsy, or maybe they were anxious to get on with the honeymoon, and were not paying attention to the road.

The car veered off the highway and smashed into a tree, killing the groom and leaving the bride with the awful task of having to report the tragedy. She walked out into the highway in order to flag someone down. There, as the bride was standing in the middle of the street, still in her wedding dress, the driver of the car that came around the corner only saw her for a split second. He hit her. As it turns out, the motorist was the best man, and he had had a bit too much alcohol himself. His reaction time was slow and he didn't even apply the brakes before the impact.

In a panic, he dragged the bride off the roadway. Thinking he had killed her, he buried her in a shallow grave. The only problem was, she wasn't quite dead at the time and being buried alive added to the unspeakable horror.

According to the legend, that's why sometimes late at night, you'll see a woman in a wedding dress wandering around in the cemetery, grieving for her lost love--desperate to avenge the unspeakable horror.

Look For Me

   With this story in mind, I paid a visit
to the old cemetery with a young woman who
was modeling for me at the time.

   Our first trip out to the cemetery was
relatively uneventful, with one exception. I
noticed that I was having trouble with my
usually reliable camera equipment. In one
case, I took a picture of the model with her
foot resting on the border of a grave marker.
The resulting image had a strange ghostly
hue. She took her foot down and the next
shot was normal. At another grave, she sat
on a very wide base of a headstone, posing
next to the actual marker. The photo came
out almost black. While I was fiddling with
my camera, trying to figure out what was
wrong, I heard the young lady apologize to
the spirits. The subsequent photo was fine.

   Normally I would just shrug my
shoulders and go on, but this wasn't our first
brush with some odd things during photo
shoots.

   I have a studio about eight or ten
miles from that cemetery, which I use for
making videos and shooting stills. Some
months prior to that, we had noticed that on
several occasions, we'd turn off the lights and
lock up for the evening, only to look back and
notice that a light was still on. I'd go back inside, turn the light off, that I was certain I
had turned off before, and lock up again. If

this had happened just once, I would not pay a whole lot of attention. But in five years, it has happened enough times to make me consider the idea, that if spirits do exist, they may have the power to affect things in the real world.

So when the camera problems happened at the cemetery, and the model apologized to the spirits and the problems vanished, it was enough to make me pay close attention.

After that, I had the idea that we should return to the cemetery and make a video documenting the experience about the camera difficulties. Little did I know at the time, that that may have been a very bad idea.

Or maybe it was good. I guess it depends upon your perspective. If you don't want to know about the possibility that spirits live beyond the flesh-and-blood life with which we are familiar, then it could have been a blunder. On the other hand, if you are open to the concept that there is life beyond what we readily see around us, then maybe it was a terrific idea.

When we returned to that cemetery to make our video, my model started sensing an entity, who she said was pacing "beyond the light" at the edge of the cemetery. I didn't feel or see anything. I'm the reporter. I kept my camera rolling and watched the model go from a perfectly composed actress to a lady totally focused on an entity that she said was grieving for a lost loved one. At first, she said she sensed that the grief was related to either a husband or a child. But then, with a little flashlight in her hand, she began searching the cemetery, zeroing in on a single grave, like a beagle after a bone.

She pointed at one marker conclusively and stated over and over, "This is it. This is it."

I was clueless. I didn't know what was happening. She tried to read the inscription on the grave and when she couldn't, she asked me if I could read it. There was no way. The marker was so old and so worn that it was just impossible, under those circumstances, to make anything out. But, there was no doubt in the young lady's mind that that grave was the object of interest to the entity that had made contact with her.

She described the woman as "not tall," with her hair up in a bun, searching, pacing, and grieving.

I'm not sure how long the entity was present--a half hour, or maybe a little longer, but eventually things calmed down and we got back to work making our video.

To be continued....

Reviews

Look For Me
Worldwide

Look For Me is a special novel that could have only been written by a man like Douglas Kirk. From Ireland to Pennsylvania; from Hollywood to Texas, this book will keep you enthralled! Real life and times interspersed with fiction keeps you wondering what's coming next. A little romance to keep the ladies happy, enough battle gore for the men. *Look For Me* is a memorable tale of a trek from one side of the world to the other. It is a thoroughly enjoyable story that starts a thousand years ago and ends today. Or does it?

--Lorraine Brandt, Texas

Look For Me is an exquisitely crafted novel. Each chapter possesses an arc of its own and reads almost like a short story in its completeness; yet the chapters add up to more than the sum of their parts.

--Dodie Bernard, Canada

Two elements that make this book exquisite: natural, flowing dialog and characters that act like real people. I feel like I've made friends with them.
--Natalie Cross, Colorado

Look For Me

Is it imagination or memory? That's what we have to ask Douglas Kirk. Where does a novelist get an idea like the one that he dreamed up and turned in to *Look For Me*? Truly unique. Truly different. Either he's got an incredible imagination, or he has a lot of explaining to do.

--Clifton Spencer, California

I just finished *Look For Me*...Wonderful! I loved it!!! I have to say that I am a sucker for happy endings, but this was truly great!!! I loved the way it was all tied together. I totally got invested in each character and was super happy with the outcome!

--Jamie Layne Stinson Arnall, Mexico

If you're Irish, read this book. You'll see that the Irish are not only the most strong-willed people in the world, but the most romantic. Don't even open *Look For Me* unless you have the time to read it in one sitting. Putting it down is impossible.

--Drew O'Henry, New York

This is such a special book. *Look For Me* opens so many doors and offers so much hope that I predict it will be discussed for a long time to come. Douglas Kirk was guided in the writing of this book. I feel it. It's not something you write on your own--not something this important. He had help. The question is, who and how?

--Gerald Carson, Kansas

Synopsis

Look For Me

When despair gives way to the desire to pull the trigger, and end it all, a chance meeting changes everything. But who is this girl, and why is it that she does what she does for a perfect stranger?

Could her actions have something to do with a thousand years, two continents and eras that are separated by centuries?

The first book in the *Look For Me* series is just the beginning.

Is it memory or imagination? That's the question Douglas Kirk kept asking himself as he wrote *Look For Me*, his incredible novel spanning a thousand years and two continents. A battle in eleventh century Ireland, an immigration ship in 1850, a coal mine in the 1870s, and 1950s Hollywood, these are the settings.

"A strange thing happened when I started writing this story," said Kirk, "I conceived the idea more than two years earlier, then had an epiphany on exactly how the plot would go. After that, I stole time from my regular work to literally just report something that seemed to flow out of my mind. I had no idea how or why, but the words just got onto paper. The characters told me what they were going to say. I was a listener, an observer. I was not in control. Within about 20 hours of writing, it was done. I was amazed." Kirk said that the idea jingled around in his head for a couple of years and was one of those stories that he couldn't dismiss.

"It kept telling itself over and over," said Kirk, "not clearly at first, but then finally, boom, it dropped on me and I had no choice but to write it."

Kirk describes *Look For Me* as a story about lovers, caught in historically accurate circumstances, struggling to go on. Written as a novel, but conceived as a motion picture, *Look For Me* is the ultimate date movie that is sure to move audiences to tears, joy, smiles, and amorous feelings. Couples will be holding hands by the end and they will never look at each other the same way again.

About The Author

Douglas Kirk

Douglas Kirk has been writing all of his adult life. He is an accomplished photographer. Kirk said when he studied at the American International High School in The Hague, Holland, that he'd be happy in life if he could be a writer and photographer.

He graduated with honors from Texas A&M University with a B.S. in Psychology, an M.S. in Experimental Psychology (specializing in learning) and a B.S. in Journalism (with a minor in photography).

He's had more than 350 articles and 500 photographs published in national magazines. He owns a community newspaper that has earned 119 awards in writing and photography, including Kirk as Photojournalist of the Year for Texas from the Houston Press Club (twice), and the Vic Mauldin Memorial Award for Advertising Photography (seven times) from the Texas Community Newspaper Association. Kirk has written twenty-five other books.